C000295441

$\mathscr{I}$N THE
$\mathscr{L}$IONS $\mathscr{M}$OUTH
AND
OTHER STORIES

ALSO AVAILABLE BY DAVID MOORE

THE ABBOT

In the Lions Mouth and Other Stories

To Thers:
Enjoy classmate

[signature]

DAVID MOORE

authorHOUSE®

AuthorHouse™
1663 Liberty Drive
Bloomington, IN 47403
www.authorhouse.com
Phone: 1-800-839-8640

© 2011 by DAVID MOORE. All rights reserved.
www.davidmoorewriter.com

No part of this book may be reproduced, stored in a retrieval system, or transmitted by any means without the written permission of the author.

These Short stories are a work of fiction and except for historical fact, any reference to any person living or dead is purely coincidental.
This book is fully the work of David Moore and is protected under copyright as such.

First published by AuthorHouse   09/27/2011

ISBN: 978-1-4670-0096-3 (sc)
ISBN: 978-1-4670-0097-0 (ebk)

Printed in the United States of America

Any people depicted in stock imagery provided by Thinkstock are models, and such images are being used for illustrative purposes only.
Certain stock imagery © Thinkstock.

This book is printed on acid-free paper.

Because of the dynamic nature of the Internet, any web addresses or links contained in this book may have changed since publication and may no longer be valid. The views expressed in this work are solely those of the author and do not necessarily reflect the views of the publisher, and the publisher hereby disclaims any responsibility for them.

———•◆•———

FOR HANNAH, BOB AND PETER. OUR FUTURE.
KEEP THE FAITH.

———•◆•———

When I began to write in earnest, I found my creative process hampered by some black, gnarled, dark force still inside me. Imagine the writing process as the opening of a door to a room filled with boxes. These boxes contain ideas, sentences, story lines and the plethora of thoughts and sayings. The writer collects things from each box, sits down and writes. In my case I had thirty years of memories, mostly police memories, not all good, in three massive boxes. Stark, heavy, unopened boxes obstructing my room doorway. Blocking the path to my imagination and inspiration.

Fed up with squeezing past the boxes, I opened them. Inside I found old demons, fears, thoughts. Many buried and dormant. From another time. A bad, war like time. A time when we hated each other and inflicted terrible pain and grief. Yet a time too of great comradeship, hope and light. In writing away my fears and memories I have completed the journey I started in nineteen seventy nine. I hope you enjoy these stories; they are so to speak, my children.

In the police short stories I have tried to show the human condition, the futility of hatred and the virtue of life. A life is a precious gift. Easily taken or destroyed beyond repair. In the other short stories, well, I have let my imagination loose. I have become the teller of tales.

David Moore
www.davidmoorewriter.com

Table of Contents

Although this story is a work of fiction I have attended
several incidents of this nature during my lifetime.

1

In the Lion's Mouth

◆

It's July. Strong summer heat mingles with the stale smell of cigarette smoke and sweat in the back of the armoured Land rover. It's pushing on for 11.30 pm. The radio crackles into life and we all listen eagerly as the message tells us of shots fired. It gives the location and asks for any callsign on this radio net close to the location to respond.

'Whiskey from 153, we'll take that,' my boss says on the radio.

Then turning to us in the rear he says, 'Get kitted up boys,' turning back to the radio he says, 'ETA about zero three over.'

Mass fumbling as three larger than average police men try to zip up fire proof overalls, pull on balaclavas and get helmets fastened, all in this small confined space. Black nylon long batons are drawn, gloves put on. The shrill wail of the siren cuts through the air like a banshee. The radio is alive with chatter as we try to hear more news. We hear callsigns who are making their way there. I imagine the chaos in their vehicles too.

Our vehicle lurches to a rocking stop and heavy armoured doors protest as they are flung open. We debus, leaving the rear of our safe haven. I am last out so I secure the doors to keep our driver safe. What a sight awaits me then.

A bonfire, fully alight. Scores of drunken revellers dancing around it, noise, smoke and two young men carrying a third man between them. He has been shot in the forehead and is quite dead. They have an arm each, draped around their necks like football scarves and they are walking. The body stands between them, stiff legged and rigid. When they walk his legs trail out behind him in a rigid protest. As they pass me by I notice the back of his head is gaping open, wet blood clotted hair sits out proud of the rest of his scalp. The exit wound. Obviously. He is indeed, quite dead. We try to get them to put him down but to no avail.

'He'll be alright mate.' One says to me 'He just has to walk it off. Know what I mean like?'

We gently take the body and lay him on his back. The crowd is surging toward us every few seconds as drunken ghouls and onlookers want to get a better view. God help us. Not exactly something you would proudly tell your grandchildren. What have we become?

The ambulance pulls in and we place the body on the gurney, helped by the two ambulance crew.

'What hospital?' I ask

'Eh,' says the driver pointing to his ears.

'What hospital?'

'Oh Belfast Royal, mate.'

With that several of the crowd surge forward and grab the body pulling it from the trolley. We grab one arm and a leg, they grab the other side and a deliberate tug of war begins. We pull and they pull. I have an arm. The body falls from the trolley all the while spilling blood and God knows what over everywhere. One of the ambulance crew, who has been holding on, suddenly has his shirt ripped open by a man in the crowd. Some fists are flying. A black nylon baton appears over my shoulder as Ryan beats a path through to the ambulance crew. The crowd reel back in a semi circle and we open the rear doors of the ambulance and deposit the gurney, complete with deceased.

Then the ambulance makes its way off to hospital. Driving across the grass, its lights flashing and sirens wailing. Soon it is lost in the sea of people. There must be at least three hundred here.

Eddie is opposite me, his tall body looks misshapen in all his public order kit. A firm hand hooks into my gunbelt from the rear. It's Ryan. He pulls me close and is shouting ;

'Don't get separated.'

'OK,' I yell back.

He looks at Eddie and shouts for him to join us. That's when I see it. A beer bottle, mid air. It seems to hang there for several seconds, then It collides with Eddie's helmet and spins off into the crowd who have now regrouped. They surge forward fuelled by drink and four hundred years of hatred. Somehow, in all this chaos, it has become the Police who have killed this young man. Many are shouting that we have not attempted to catch the killers; that we are working with the gunmen; that we are indeed to blame for this death.

There can be no logic that a drunken, hate filled mob can process at this time. We have just become the enemy. We are very, very outnumbered.

It begins in earnest.

We are taking bottles and all other missiles. I use my nylon baton, but I can't swing it fully. A fist punches my helmet. I strike out hitting another clenched fist. I feel his fingers break under the force of my baton. I'm pushing, pulling twisting and turning all shapes trying to avoid that contact. Too late. At last. Big contact on my visor. Beer bottle. Glass and wet beer hit my cheeks. The smell of the beer is almost overpowering. My visor steams up and I cannot see a thing. My breath is coming in great gasps. I'm grabbed from the front by two men. Ryan's black baton strikes over the top of me again. One man falls away his face bleeding. I hit my attacker with my baton. I'm holding it at both ends with two hands and I punch it into his face. Again and again. I feel his nose break, I see his blood. I am now fighting for my life. He too falls away.

Now I can swing my baton fully. I lash out, again and again. I can feel the solid thump as I contact with people. More stuff hits me. Another bottle. Another fist. Is this never going to end? Ryan keeps his tight grip on my belt. He pulls me with him as he too fights. We are like some Siamese twins, one cannot move without the others consent. Eddie is with us now and we are retreating to the Land rover.

Then it happens. A very heavy missile collides with my helmet. I'm dizzy. My vision blurs and I feel sick. Then the whole situation goes into slow motion for me. I see drunken, hate filled, people. Dancing around the fire. The fire where only minutes beforehand a human sacrifice was made. I am in the mouth of the beast. I can smell his breath. I can feel his malevolence. He is here. Death, demon, devil, whatever you choose to call him. HE IS HERE.

I am terrified, deep in my soul I feel his blackness. I stare into the crowd. They dance on still, chanting their songs. God help us what have we become?

Then I'm gone. Pulled out of the crowd by more police. I take shelter from all the incoming behind a shield held by another officer. Simon fires his baton gun right beside me. I smell the rotten egg stench that comes with the discharge. He is reloading. I look back and see the crowd begin to evaporate.

'That's the way' I say to myself 'Atta boy Simon'.

I stand at the back of the Land Rover with Eddie and Ryan. A large bottle of water is being passed around. We all drink deeply. Alive again. I'm blessed. I really am blessed. My hands are trembling as the adrenaline begins to ebb. Eddie and I are both drenched in beer. We laugh. A nervous, boyish, laugh.

Later that night I pull on my anorak and drive home. I am exhausted and have not changed out of my overalls. I smell of stale beer and woodsmoke. At my home I make a coffee and open my patio doors. Standing out the back, in the calm morning air, I examine my boots. I turn the hosepipe on and hose away the blood and gore on my right sole. I watch it swirl down the metal drain. This was someone's life blood only a few hours ago. It pumped around his body. He laughed, drank, ate; He existed. This blood was his. Now it was in my drain.

I drink my coffee and am left alone to wrestle with my demons. The one thing that never ceases to amaze me is how cruel we can be to each other.

Ryan left the Police after this incident. He trained as a minister and now takes sermons. He, like myself, had attended one incident too many. He never said but I know he felt the Beast that night too. I could see it in him.

Eddie and I struggled on for a few months. He went off on sick leave a few weeks before I did. He died in hospital from cancer two years later. I visited him a few days before he died. The Doctor told me he would not see any visitors and I was turned away. As I walked off the Doctor caught up with me. Eddie wanted to see me. I scrubbed up. He looked awful. Ravaged by cancer, pale and thin. We said a lot to each other without speaking. That knowing silence that men such as us share. I held his hand. He told me to 'put myself right' and he would meet me on the other side. Far away from the beast.

I went to bits at his funeral, although I was surprised how long I had managed to keep it together. My own demons have, for the most part, been put to bed for the time being.

Sometimes I drink coffee on my patio and I wonder, 'What have I become?'

I spent a long time in the traffic police. Apart from those who do the job, I think, no one else knows how close officers become, nor the type of situations we can find ourselves in during the working day.

2

Nailed

———— •◆• ————

I'M A TRAFFIC OFFICER. HAVE been for ever it seems. That's right, the ticket guy, the one with the speed gun that spoils your day when you happen to be late for work or are taking the kids to school. Boo, hiss, I can hear everyone shout. Yeah, yeah, heard it all before. There are times, however, when you are glad to see me. Like the time you have broken down on the motorway and I happen along and get you a recovery vehicle and contact your work or partner, telling them that you will be late for work, or home soon. The times when I keep talking to you when the fire service are cutting the roof off your car to extract you. I'm the guy who tells you it will be alright. Sometimes I even hold your hand if you ask me to, I walk with you to the ambulance. I even get to see you in the morgue as you begin the journey to the river Styx and the meeting with the ferryman. So I suppose it's not all tickets and stern lectures.

There is a price. That's right. You sometimes have to pay a high price, I too have had to pay a price over the years. A heavy one at that. It makes me think about life and death and where we all fit into the giant jigsaw puzzle. I remember listening to the police radio chatter as a local station car chased a gang of armed robbers through a busy housing estate in Belfast. My partner and I had joined in the chase. There is something basic and necessary in a chase. Something that man has been put on the earth to fulfil. He is back to his roots, back to the beginning of existence, back to the hunter gatherer. The thrill of the chase. I could hear the mixture of fear and excitement on the radio as I listened intently, trying to glean any direction of travel and work out how to intercept the offenders. We stop short of a main road junction and then a small hatchback car speeds past the front of our vehicle. A split second later an armoured police car speeds past. We glance briefly at each other and join the hunt. Now at last we have seen the prey and have joined to swell the pack hunting it. We are talking loudly, like excited schoolboys, there is a euphoric feeling which has descended into our vehicle and is rising every second the chase continues.

For a few brief seconds we lose sight of it and that's when the gunshot rings out. Just around the next corner the hatchback has crashed and the patrol car has stopped. An officer stands, ashen faced, smoking service revolver in his hands. A man lies in the road several feet away, beside him a black pistol and a white cotton money bag. We debus from our traffic car and sprint toward the crashed vehicle. Two terrified youths are inside. There is a lot of shouting and yelling and pointing of firearms. This is the danger time. Anyone of us could be shot by the robbers or by other police. I watch as the other two men are handcuffed and their vehicle is searched. Another pistol, ski masks, more money bags and other paraphernalia are brought from the car. My partner rushes past me carrying the large first aid kit that our motorway patrol is issued with. I am brought to my senses by the sight of this familiar object and go to help.

That's when I see it. It is up close and very personal. Death. He's not quite here yet but I feel he is waiting in the wings. His shadowy figure in the background. Waiting. Watching. There is a young man on his back just beside the kerb. His body is shaking and twisting. He is fitting. There is blood everywhere. How can someone bleed this much? His eyes are staring skyward and are empty and dull. A district nurse appears as if by magic and begins to assist the police officer who has been working on him for several minutes. I notice the blood is almost black. Arterial blood. My partner and I exchange glances. He shakes his head and I nod slightly. We have seen it before and we know that the grim reaper awaits. Old Grimmie. No ferryman for this guy just yet. No pennies required.

He gives a sigh and his body goes limp. The police officer rips his shirt open and begins the process of CPR, the nurse, still kneeling starts to breath into his mouth. I can see her looking along his chest when she pauses. Looking to see if it is rising and falling on its own. I fear that is a negative. An ambulance arrives, bringing with it a trolley, a red bag full of more medical equipment and the defibrillator. We call the defibrillator the 'jump leads' in the trade. I watch as he is hooked up and charged then injected and bagged. The green plastic bag with the mask attached is strapped over his head and he is carted off to the ambulance. I can almost see the Grim Reaper climbing into the ambulance too.

We return to the nearest local police station along with several other callsigns who have attended the incident.

Coffee and statements follow along with notebook entries and a plethora of other paperwork. The officer who fired his weapon is taken from our group. He has not spoken since the incident and I assume will be sent home after the police doctor has examined him. God help him because he is a victim too. Having only a split second to decide what action to take. Imagine facing an armed robber, imagine facing a pistol, imagine the dreams and 'what if's' he will have to face in the future. A very sobering thought. Leaving the station we make a joint command decision that it is lunch time. It is actually well past lunch time and knowing the police canteens will all be closed it is decided a drive through at the local fast food outlet, is in order.

So an extraordinary morning turns into an ordinary afternoon. We know our traffic bosses will want a de-brief and a blow by blow account of the action or inaction that we had taken. At the drive through window a spotty faced youth takes our order. Several minutes later we are parked in a secluded spot away from the public eye and we try eating. No one is hungry. There is another strange thing too, complete silence. There has hardly been a word spoken since we left the station. I drop my burger back into its multi-coloured box and look over at my partner.

'Trev.'

'What mate?'

'If I get shot don't ever let me die in the gutter. Put me in the back of the car.'

'What if you die in the car?'

'I won't mind. Just don't let it be in the gutter.'

'OK Dave.'

'Promise?'

'Promise.'

Trevor and I have been partners for three or four years and are very close. It's a strange bond. Some days we fight, most days we laugh. We share secrets that no one else knows. Not our families, nor our wives, no one. I know he will keep his promise to me as I will to him. There is a sharing between us. As well as food and equipment and all tangible things we share a knowing. A relationship such as ours is forged in life's furnace and can never be split apart or reduced. Even now, years later, we still have that sharing and are at ease in each others company when we meet. We speak little of the past and only pick the good stuff. That is how life's defence mechanism works. I suppose.

———•◆•———

Like I said at the start, life is precious. We should cherish it. Some, however, find it all too much. We should never judge or condemn, just be there, be respectful and get the job done. Just get the job done.

———•◆•———

3

New Day

THE HOUSE IS A SMALL terrace type. What the estate agents call a mid-terrace. A concrete walkway leads to the front door and cuts the small front garden in half. Not that there is much of a garden. Just patches of grass some more yellow than others and the flower beds, now overgrown, tell a tale of care and planting but not lately. Not for several years. Weeds fight with the remaining plants to get light and the best from the long dead soil. A metal handle adjacent to the front door suggests to me that an elderly person has been the tenant before this one. It's just positioned to assist older legs up the small, cement step and into the narrow hall.

I'm greeted at the door into the kitchen by a Paramedic. His smart green overalls and neat work belt tell me his shift has only just started. Just like mine. There is a large green bag sitting just inside the kitchen door.

'She's out the back officer,' he stammers, eyes dropping to scan the un-swept floor.

I nod and push through the tiny kitchen, passing the cold kettle and the small drop leaf table at which sits the second ambulance man. He is a lot younger and pale around the face and neck. As I enter the back yard I know I will have to turn and look up. I don't want to. I really don't. I can feel the dead eyes stare at me before I am fully in the yard. I see a metal dustbin and an unused push mower leaning against the wall. An old car battery and a faded yellow gas cylinder sit side by side. I notice the grass in the small area at the rear of the yard is in worse condition than the front garden. I must look up. I know I have to. It's my duty.

My gaze scans the outside wall and begins to climb skyward. Several grey plastic waste pipes run at angles from the upstairs bathroom. They join a main, larger, grey, waste pipe and are fused together as one. I see brown boots. Scuffed toe caps point earthward. The socks are black and red in horizontal bands and disappear into faded blue denim jeans. She is wearing a plain white smock type blouse, hands down by her sides. I look at the face. She is a middle aged lady. Her head is kinked to the right and her tongue is protruding, all purple and swollen. This is indeed the stuff of nightmares. I cannot see the noose but the rope is taut and is going into the back bedroom window. She has been dead a long time. Several hours at least.

Noises in the house make me look back at the kitchen. A fire officer, complete with white helmet and rubber boots is pushing past the ambulance crew. He meets me in the garden. Looking up as he leaves the safety of the kitchen he exclaims;

'God in heaven!'

Then shaking his head he asks me,' OK to cut her down?'

'Aye, go ahead, but don't cut the knot. Can you cut about a foot above her head?'

'Sure Constable. Dear God, poor wee woman.'

He returns to the house, as do I. In the small front room I hear him briefing the fire crew. He is telling them what to expect and he finishes by saying that anyone who does not wish to see this can go wait in the fire truck. No one does, what brave men we have in our fire service.

Leaving them to take her down, I climb the stairs. Her bedroom door is slightly ajar. Entering it there is a strange silence, almost a peacefulness. It's as if the wee house is in mourning too. This house has probably seen her in deep depression, joyful happiness, sorrow and a plethora of other senses and feelings all of which have led her to take this step. On her dressing table sits an envelope. Propped up between a brass candlestick and a small bottle of perfume. There are items of jewellery arranged in a neat row. It's as if they are waiting for their owner to return and wear them, choose them, justify them again. Two rings, a bracelet, an amulet type of wristband and a delicate lady's watch.

I open the note and read it. It's a simple, sorry, addressed to JB. It reads; 'I'm sorry JB. It's all been too much what with Jack away and now Rita too. Forgive me. I will see you again. All my love Brenda.'

I drop the letter into my clear plastic evidence bag and seal it. I have left it open so the CID can read it without having to handle it. The envelope I tuck in behind it. My attention is drawn to the rope. It has been tied around the wooden bed end. There are several twists through the wooden rails. I imagine her testing it, pulling on it, before finally being content that it would hold her weight. The whole bed has been pushed against the wall and the window jammed open. A long wooden stick has been jammed into the window frame and is holding the window. I see a nail through one end of the stick and into the sill. Casting my gaze around the room I see a hammer and a small plastic tub of assorted nails sitting on top of the small television. The tub is yellow and it says 'Cocca Butter' on the side. Nails and screws are scattered inside it in profusion. Suddenly the rope goes slack. I hear the scrape of an aluminium ladder being drawn along the outside wall. I leave the bedroom. A police photographer will have to photograph the window and the bedstead before I can seize the rope. I close the bedroom door and as I begin to walk away I pause at the second bedroom. Opening the door I am greeted by a musty smell that tells me this bedroom is not used much. From the bed I pull a red woollen blanket and fold it over my arm.

In the front room the fire men have placed the lady on the black vinyl settee. I notice she is red haired and has makeup still on. I place the blanket over her, covering her completely. Dignity in death is still very important. Someone may arrive to identify her, or a neighbour may call unwittingly, so she needs covered. Mainly it's to stop her looking at me. Her eyes are open. She has a Mona Lisa look. A strange, grotesque, yet still feminine look. In later years I remember how she looked. I wanted her to know that I did all that I could to preserve her privacy and protect her from the ghouls.

In the front garden the fire men are smoking and standing in silence. I offer a well done lads type speech and am greeted with nods and eyes that look everywhere but at me. I note the name of the senior fire chief there for my scene log. My ambulance crew are long gone. I await the arrival of the local Doctor to pronounce life extinct before I can get the undertaker to collect. On the back of the scene log I tick off procedures completed and note some still to do. In the front room I pull up a chair and sit with the body. I will stay with her until she is taken from me. That way she won't be alone, won't be at the mercy of the world which was too much for her. Perhaps then she won't call to visit when I'm old and alone in bed in the wee small hours. We sit in silence and listen the ticking clock inside, and the world waking up outside, and beginning its new day.

I served for a number of years in a border station. These were often remote and in areas hostile to police, open to attacks and ambushes. A lot of my time there was spent on patrol with various regiments of the British Army. We seem to have walked a lot.

4

So We Walk and Walk.

————•◆•————

I T'S MID WINTER IN MY border station. Frozen ground and biting cold make working a lot more difficult. I'm at the nearby army base waiting in a dusty, stale, briefing room. Wearing my thermal long johns and matching vest underneath my police uniform. Sweating mildly as the room begins to fill with soldiers. I've completed a dozen of these patrols. Eagle patrols; an army name. We refer to them in the briefing as EP's. We board the helicopter and are dropped off at certain locations where we carry out vehicle check points and foot patrols, searches and observations against an unseen, unknown enemy. A ghost enemy. An enemy who attacks with booby trap devices, sniper shootings and the odd face to face fire fight. Always watching, gathering information, targeting us as we in turn target them. Cat and mouse, as it has been for the last twenty five years.

An intelligence officer brings us up to speed with what has been going on in the area of our operations to-day. I'm hearing things in more detail. Things I've only heard mentioned in passing at the older police briefings given over the last few weeks. My regiment I am patrolling with to-day is the Argyll and Sutherland Highlanders. ASH as they are known in military circles. Half the team being briefed will be dropped off first by helicopter and will complete a foot patrol. I am in the second squad. I will be in and out of the helicopter all day as it picks me up and deposits me at chosen locations close to and on the border with the Irish Republic. I am introduced to the patrol commander, a surly Scot, on his fourth tour in Ulster. He is a corporal. We shake hands and he sits beside me. Introducing himself as John. Although I have never worked with him before I know the drill. I'm in charge of the details obtained at the vehicle check points and I'm responsible in the event of a member of the public making a complaint against any military personnel. If we get involved in a terrorist incident, a contact, as the army call it, the patrol commander takes over and I follow his direction. The normal rule is that I stay with the GPMG team and return fire at any targets I can clearly identify as a threat. GPMG is the general purpose machine gun carried by one patrol member. It is large and hangs on a webbing type strap around the soldier. There is a canvas bag attached to the side of the weapon, containing the ammunition. The weapon is belt fed so other members of the patrol carry ammunition belts in the event that the GPMG requires feeding. I've seen them being fired and they are very greedy indeed.

I can see from the outset that this patrol is slightly different. There is a soldier joining us who is not ASH. He is older and carry's a different weapon. A Colt M16 assault rifle. We know it as an Armalite. The rest of the weapons are standard SLR's. Big, heavy semi automatics firing a large seven point six two round. They are a real man stopper but are heavy, unlike the nimble Colt. As for me I carry my trusty Ruger Mini 14 rifle. I have four magazines in two green pouches on my utility belt as well as my Ruger magnum pistol and its thirty rounds. It sounds like a lot of ammunition but in a contact situation the guns will rapidly dispose of the rounds at an amazing rate. So I have been told.

Now we walk to the small concrete loading bay and the military load their rifle's in groups of three, supervised by the patrol commander. I load mine too and allow him to check it. Although he has no control over my weapon he is the patrol commander and good gun manners dictate that I give him his place, after all he is responsible for the rest of the men in the group.

Now there is a last minute change of plan. We are told that one of the soldiers is to stay behind to allow our new friend to join us. I'm told that there has been a radical change to our tasks and am offered the opportunity to stay behind too. I decline and am greeted with nods and smiles. The stranger nods at me too. I have a feeling I know who he is or at least what he is. The green, grey and black Lynx attack helicopter arrives, gliding onto the heli-pad with all the grace of a ballerina. The metal skids kiss the tarmac and we run, stooped like old men, and are soon aboard. The smell of aviation fuel coupled with the whupp whupp of the rotor blades and the mini tornado of dust and debris being kicked up tells me I am airborne. Everything vibrates. I sit with my rifle pointing skyward, trapped between my knees. A mixture of adrenaline, fear and intrigue running through my body. At last we are flying.

Ulster hedge rows and copse's of trees unfold just under our belly. We are low, very, very low and are travelling faster than normal. We track the road running parallel to the

Irish Republic. The patrol commander turns holding up his thumb, then three fingers. Telling us we are landing in three minutes. He is wearing headphones and is in contact with the pilot. Pilots are cool, wearing green crash helmets and aviator sun glasses. There are names stencilled on their helmets in yellow. This one says Capt 'Markie' Marks and has a Donald Duck underneath it. I think this is something we have picked up from our American cousins, rather like the cartoons drawn on the nose of the Flying Fortresses in the last war.

Our Lynx kisses the green field very briefly and I jump out onto the wet grass. I can see soldiers kneeling and aiming rifles at unseen targets, covering the metal bird until it has gone. It is gone in seconds. Flown into the empty sky and we are alone. Vulnerable and alone. Our new friend is talking to the corporal, pointing and gesticulating with his arms. I notice he carries very little equipment, just a small daysack and kidney pouches. On the other hand the corporal and his team are loaded like shire horses, heavy packs, ammunition belts and all the rest.

We walk along the road. Strung out in two lines with good spaces between the men. Soldiers at the front sometimes stop, allowing the rest to pass, covering always covering each other. An array of military equipment is on display, the Violet Joker, the White Sifter and the faithful Clansman radio. All look the same, designed to confuse snipers. We are open to snipers in this area, the same men who planted a bomb at a cenotaph on remembrance Sunday, killing civilians, who attacked and mercilessly gunned down worshipers at a Baptist meeting house and who have killed, maimed and bombed in the name of freedom. I shiver at the thoughts in my head.

No cars approach. It is way too quiet for my liking. Our slick, well disciplined patrol now changes direction at a fork in the road. I know the right fork leads us to the Irish Republic in a few hundred yards. We take it. After a few steps we begin to take to the fields again. This is different. Walking parallel to the main road that we have just left we stop where the road bends sharply left and runs over a small stream. Our new friend gives some silent hand signals and the patrol scatters to different areas of the field. Again all round cover is provided without speech or talking, professional, well practiced drills. I am kneeling beside the GPMG crew as instructed. My heart is thumping and my breathing is very shallow. I'm listening, but I don't know what for. Waiting, watching, but why?

Our new friend is walking toward me, crouched, long strides he looks determined and resolute. Kneeling in front of me he says;

'Davy, we are meeting friendlies here'.

'OK', I reply.

'It's all good, no matter what they look like they are ours'.

We both nod and smile. He is a lot older than the rest. At least late thirties and there is a distinct Home Counties twang in his voice. With that he is gone, scurrying off across the field toward the far hedgerow. That's when I see them. A tall man in combat clothing emerges from the hedge. He has an M16 also and I notice it has a grenade launcher attached. As I watch three more men appear. Two are similar in appearance, dressed in jeans and green Barbour jackets and carrying AK47's, but the third, well,he is wearing a Gillie suit. I am astounded. I've seen pictures of these suits in books, but to see one in the flesh is truly amazing. He looks like a walking bush. There are brown and black strips of cloth hanging from the suit, interspersed with small branches and leaves. A sniper. I notice he carries some sort of bolt action rifle. All are now whispering to our older friend.

My corporal now joins me.

'Davy, there is a landmine about three hundred meters past the road bend. We are to stay here while these boys defuse it. Ok?'

I nod.

'Who is that guy with us?' I ask.

'He's the covert ATO. The other boys have followed the command wire into Donegal and have been there for three days, they think the Provo's have abandoned it. We'll just sit tight.'

Our new friend and two other lads from the hedgerow now slowly make their way into the distance. I am signalled forward by the corporal and end up at the hedgerow. I watch the three men until they drop into the drainage ditch and are gone from view. I dealt with a car accident on this road not long ago and am frantically trying to imagine where the culvert may be.

A light tap on my leg makes me jump. I turn to see 'tree man' beside me, complete with gillie suit. He points to my radio and silently mouths 'Off.' I turn the volume knob anticlockwise until I hear the familiar click. As I look back at him I nod and he winks. We wait. Then we wait some more.

After what seems like an absolute age the corporal turns to me signalling that I can eat. Two other men get the signal too. I've never done this before, we normally take a break and all eat together. I suppose this makes sense, some eating some keeping watch. Swinging my knapsack off my back I remove the flask of hot coffee and the box of sandwiches. The coffee smell fills my nostrils as the brown liquid swirls in the cup. I feel I am being watched. Glancing to my right tree man is watching me, or to be more accurate watching the coffee. I offer the cup and he accepts. His hands are black with dirt and grime. There is mud under his fingernails. He drinks quickly and quietly. My sandwich is refused by a shake of the head and the empty cup is returned with a broad smile. Nothing forges friendships like a cup of hot coffee. Not a word has been spoken; however a bond has been formed. I admire the dedication and determination of these men.

Several hours later the three amigo's return from the direction of the culvert. As they approach there is a silent 'stand to' issued and everyone is very still, straining for the faintest sound or slightest movement beyond the men's return. Our ATO has defused the landmine.

'Davy, here is the grid for the device, call it in on your radio, say that you have found a group of milk churns and request ATO.' says the corporal.

Turning on my radio I do as I have been asked, while I am transmitting the corporal is transmitting too, on the military net. Finishing my transmission I hear the familiar sound of an approaching helicopter. My new friends, the ATO, tree man and the rest are disappearing through the hedgerow on our right. Into the adjoining field. Several seconds later a large Puma helicopter touches down, the men board and all are gone in an instant. We are now being split into two groups and deployed along the road. I stay at this side of the culvert while half the patrol walk across the fields and secure the far side of the road.

More helicopters land, more soldiers and eventually two military Transit Vans turn up. I recognise these as bomb disposal or ATO from Omagh. I had worked with them several weeks ago at an unexploded under car booby trap device. Milk churns are loaded into the vans and a command wire, detonators and all the paraphernalia bomb makers use is carefully bagged and taken away for forensic examination.

After everyone has gone we are left with the corporal and the original patrol that I had started out with that morning.

'Well Davy, big day, eh?'

'Aye surely.' How are we getting back, helicopter?'

'Shanks mare', he says pointing to his boots, 'flying hours all used up I'd say'.

So we walk. Cold, alone and still trying to be alert. At a cross roads two miles from the culvert the corporal stops and we take up defensive positions. Our corporal says;

'Listen up, covert van ETA zero five, right here.' He glances at me and smiles. We await the arrival of a plain coloured Transit van and an army driver in civilian clothing. In the blacked out, dark rear of the van I reflect on my day. My 'find' would be on the six o'clock news; my parents would hear where it was and wonder if I was near it. Just how near it they would never know, all in all it's been a good result. Our van lurches and bounces as we head home, uncomfortable? Oh yes, but at least it beats walking.

Again I have tried to capture the mixture of excitement and danger in policework.

5

The Arrest;

—— ◆ ——

IT'S THE TAIL END OF the summer and what a summer it has been. I have attended more sectarian attacks on private houses than I ever thought possible. Windows smashed, petrol bombs thrown at front doors, cars burned out in driveways, heating oil tanks set alight and slogans daubed on walls. The two tribes have excelled themselves, so much for the peace process.

I'm on mobile patrol with the military, a turn of duty which I quite like. The Royal regiment of Fusiliers all dressed in full combats and wearing the beret with the red and white plume attached to the cap badge. It looks like a bottle brush on their caps and when they run, which is often, it draws attention like no other item. It's like the white rump of a deer or a rabbit's tail, always caught in the peripheral vision and man as a natural hunter is drawn to its unique movement. The Major at the briefing had asked them to wear the beret and not the Kevlar helmet. He said it would add an air of normality to the patrol, what with the peace process and all in full implementation. That particular statement was somewhat lost on me as the sight of sixteen squadies, faces blackened, SA80's at the ready, running from doorway to doorway does little to suggest peace. However, that is how we were at this present time.

My bosses were using the military to deliver policing on the cheap. They were patrolling the estates where sectarian attacks were very likely. A new term called 'sectarian interface' had been coined, it basically meant an area where the tribal boundaries met. There were a lot of buzz words and big phrases used to mean the three hundred years of hatred boiled over at these points. For the layman or foreign traveller the tribal colours normally painted on the kerbstones changed along with any murals or flags draped from lamp posts. Although the reason why any traveller would choose to visit here escapes me.

So we mount up, climbing into the green army land rovers. The top hatch is flung open and a soldier stands up on with a leg on each rear seat. His top half protruding through the opening. He is the 'top cover' his job to return fire first when an attack goes in. A lonely and not very popular job as you can imagine. I sit half way along the seat between two Geordies and am fascinated by their accents. This is their fourth tour of Northern Ireland and they are giving a history lesson to a younger squaddie. I feel deeply embarrassed as my country is laid bare and depicted as a savage and brutal land. One says;

'And it's no like bein doon the toon in Newcastle man. Naw, naw. Here they all want ta kill ya like.'

The young, wide eyed squaddie, looks at me open mouthed. He nods and asks stupid questions which the other two reply to. They compare it to Kosovo and Bosnia. I hang my head.

My country, the country which built the greatest ships in the world. The country that designed the ejector seat, the Harrier jump jet, the agricultural tractor. The country that gave the world the greatest footballer ever, the first proper heart surgeon and a host of scholars, poets and writers. I sit quietly.

My police radio crackles into life and an 'All callsigns,' broadcast begins. It appears that a man and woman have been attacked by a youth with a pistol on the Main Street. The man has been beaten around the head and face, a description of the youth is circulated and the last known direction of travel given. I tell the patrol commander, a corporal, where we need to be and he relays the information over his military radio. Soon we stop at a garage forecourt and debuss.

The patrol gathers around me and I relay the information I already have. There are a row of tall, Victorian houses across the street, complete with small front gardens and an alleyway at the rear. The soldiers are despatched in pairs to search the gardens and alley. I watch as their bottle brushes bob and weave across the busy road. I decide to check behind the garage and the scattered shops making up this area. A DVD rental shop, a chippy, a convenience store and a now closed hairdressers. Lifting my large Dragon lamp I walk around to the grass area at the rear of the shops. I am alone and enjoy the peace and quiet for a few seconds, I work better on my own as there are less distractions and no one else to look out for.

I illuminate the grass area and scan the broad bright beam along in a slow arc. A red object catches my eye and I return the lamp briefly, hovering on it for a few seconds. It's a body, in the grass not twenty yards from me. I draw my Ruger pistol with my right hand and shout.

'Armed police. Stand up. Do it now!'

To my total astonishment a tall skinny youth stands up.

'Put your hands up,' I yell, and he does as I have asked him. That is when I see it, a black pistol protruding from the waistband of his trousers. Oh no. It's him alright.

'Hands up. Walk toward me. Do it now!'

'Don't shoot. It's cool, don't shoot!'

I look at my pistol and find I have managed to cock it with my right thumb. How did I do that? The voice in my head is telling me to keep my front sight clear and my target blurred. I am following its instruction to the letter. This is my worst nightmare. Worse than a cot death, a house fire or fatal road crash. The sweat runs down my cheeks and I am still shouting, although it seems to be the same thing over and over.

'Do it now.' Seems to be all I can manage to say.

He stops a few yards from me. I can see the pistol is a Walther P99, black and cold looking. If he chooses to draw now I will be outgunned and we both know it. I have the edge at the minute by keeping him covered. His eyes are transfixed on my magnum pistol.

'With your left hand remove the pistol and drop it!'

'Don't shoot mister, please don't shoot!'

'Do it now!' I yell, can I not think of something more constructive to say? No, it seems I am stuck with this phrase. A hand draws the Walther, I hold my breath. This is it. Will I shoot? Oh God please help me.

The pistol clatters to the ground a few feet from me. I let out a long breath.

'You any other weapons?' I enquire.

'Another pistol around my back.'

'Same again, draw it and throw it to me. Do it now.' Oh there I go again.

He gingerly removes another gun, a small silver air pistol and it hits the ground. How could I have found the only man in Britain who had two guns on him? I make him turn around and place his hands on the back of his head. Suddenly there is the clatter of running feet people pushing past me. I am startled momentarily and I feel myself jump but then I see the bottle brushes and hear the excited voices.

'Zulu Alfa one zero this is Alfa,' says a Geordie voice, 'RUCLO has detained one gunman . . . . no shots fired . . . . weapons recovered . . . . over.'

I holster up and handcuff my prisoner from behind. A search reveals a set of brass knuckles in his coat pocket and a knife. It's not a large Rambo type combat knife but it is still capable of spoiling your whole day none the less.

After he is booked in to the custody suite I go for a coffee and to write a notebook entry. I will have to fill out a' service weapon drawn' form for headquarters to read. If they think it not justified I will be prosecuted by the police and could lose my job, did you ever hear such a thing? Some office bound officer will decide my fate. Someone who was not there and may not have served on the streets for years. My hands are so trembling that I have trouble holding the cup. The kitchen door opens and it's my boss. He sets both guns on the table along with the empty evidence bags and makes a joke about how it could only happen to me. We both laugh, I know I almost shot a youth tonight and he knows he could now have been telling my wife how I died and what a courageous officer I was and how she should be proud. I pick up the Walther and unload it. It is the real thing; I count out the nine millimetre rounds and place them and it in the evidence bag. I complete the front of the bag and put my initials on the top corner. DM 1. My evidence. My arrest.

The patrol commander and another soldier come to the kitchen and shake hands with me. They don't say much, thank me for the patrol and both look at the walther in the bag. I know they will have to log everything for their bosses and they need to know the gun was real and loaded. As they turn to leave the corporal looks back over his shoulder and says;

'Well done mate. Nice arrest'.

The youth I arrested was suffering from a mental breakdown. He was only about nineteen or twenty and was eventually sent to a secure hospital for treatment. I often wondered what became of him and why I never fired my gun. My psychiatrist says it was my training kicking in, my wife says it's because I'm too nice. I will go with the wife's decision on this one.

---◆---

It was just after Christmas and my wife and I were walking the dogs in the local forest. There was very deep snow and in the white landscape I began to wonder what would happen if it just kept snowing and snowing and snowing . . . .

---◆---

6

Smoking Kills

— ◆ —

I STOP. DEAD IN MY tracks. There; just there; right in front of me lies a cigarette packet. Embassy Red. A twenty pack. Still wrapped in the factory cellophane. Incredible. I could not recall the last time I'd seen this. Cigarettes; real factory cigarettes. Gold dust, the Holy Grail, the number of nights I'd dreamt of lighting a factory cigarette. I even carry a Zippo lighter all the time in the event of this momentous occasion happening. I can almost hear the dry, crisp crackle, as the virgin white stick of tobacco ignites. Almost smell the smoke and feel it drawing into my mouth and lungs. Burning, caressing, stimulating. Almost see it curling from my nostrils as I exhaled. Oh joy. Now here it was, right here, right now.

Crouching low, I kneel down. My knees sinking several inches into the fresh snow. I can feel it crunch as it firms up beneath my weight. Slipping off my mittens I reach up to the Bolle snow goggles and push them up off my face and onto my brow. Grabbing the leather sling I slide my shotgun from my shoulder. I check the immediate area. The snow is undisturbed. Trees on my right trailing off into the distance. To my left, emptiness. Just emptiness and snow. Always snow.

I lived twenty miles north east of Belfast all my life. I remember the first day the snow came. It was the second of October. Television and radio stations were surprised as weathermen everywhere tried to explain its appearance so early and unannounced. It snowed for several days. Non stop. At first kids played as schools were closed and lovers walked hand in hand in snow covered fields and parks. Road agencies sent snow ploughs and lorry loafs of grit as they battled to keep main roads open. It snowed some more. Three weeks later it was still snowing. Temperatures plummeted at night to minus twenty in some areas. After six weeks the government declared a state of emergency. Army and police co-ordinated food drops to country areas and farmers frantically tried to feed livestock. Gas and oil companies began to struggle as householders and businesses began demanding more heating oil. Central heating fuel doubled in price. No one fully understood. No one could see that money was obsolete. More snow. Roads became impassable and abandoned vehicles were strewn everywhere.

Ten weeks into it the supermarkets were running out of food. Icebergs were sighted in the Irish Sea and Belfast Lough. A passenger ferry collided with one and sank just off the Maidens lighthouse near Larne. Ship deliveries became less and less frequent. Electricity supplies stopped as lines collapsed and the main power stations ran out of fuel. No planes had flown in weeks. Still it snowed. Reports were widespread that citizens had raided ASDA and Tesco's. Some looted televisions and white goods while the more sensible took food and supplies. Police fired baton rounds to keep crowds away but the sheer numbers of people overwhelmed them. Several fatal shootings happened. Citizens shot police and eventually law and order collapsed. Gangs of armed people looted dwelling houses, hospitals, factories. Food and fuel replaced money. Householders grouped together, fortifying homes as best they could. Oil tanks were raided. Still it snowed. Night temperatures now dropped to minus thirty and day temperatures were sometimes little higher.

I stayed home with my wife and two sons. It was the middle of July and I was foraging, with my wife, when we came upon an abandoned police car. The dead crew had been stripped of weapons and equipment long ago. Forcing the trunk open I liberated the shotgun I now carry. I had to break the lock open and the effort required, made the car move violently. The grass ledge supporting it gave way and as the car toppled into the field, the front wing caught my wife throwing her across the snow. Landing heavily I heard her scream. I knew before I turned that this was not good. Her hip was broken. I wrestled her onto the wooden sled. The homemade sled that I trailed everywhere with me. She was very cold when I brought her home. I remember cradling her head, stroking her blonde hair. Telling her it was alright.

Unable to get medical help and kept indoors by a sudden temperature drop I watched her die. Two weeks later my two boys went foraging and never returned. I never knew what happened to them, but I have a fair idea. My trips to Larne became less frequent. Some citizens had set up a barter system. Trading oil or petrol for food or clothing. My last trip found the streets deserted and frozen bodies everywhere. I can only assume that a larger party came raiding. The town was virtually unrecognisable as the deep snow covered everything. Steps had been cut here and there and aluminium ladders allowed people to climb down into the old town. It was dark and creepy in the town and so I decided to remain topside, live in my house four miles away and keep away from people.

So October rolled around again. It snowed. Not every day, but most days. I ran a petrol generator to keep two lights on in my house. I lived in one room. I slept with one eye open all the time having the fear that raiders would come. January came, so did February. It snowed. My foraging took me further and further away and one evening I got caught in a blizzard. There were few blizzards. Only three or four every year, but this was the worst one. I took shelter in an abandoned pub which was five miles from home. It was completely stripped of everything. Bringing my sled into the bar I took my tent and sleeping bag out and camped indoors. Screams in the night woke me. I lay clutching my shotgun. At first light I packed up. Before I left I checked the back room. My blood ran cold. Bodies, or to be more exact, body parts were strewn everywhere. I though it was an animal attack as packs of dogs roamed the snowy wasteland. Rumours of bear attacks were common too. Some said that Polar bears escaped from Belvue Zoo, some thought they came from the north, walking across the ice. Wherever they came from does not really matter. I had seen bears, brown bears, at the Glenwherry Bridge several weeks ago. Pressing further inside I found my answer. On the pool table. A body. A human body. Freshly butchered. Knives, cleavers, meat hooks. Butchers paraphernalia. So the cannibal rumours were true. Walking out the back door I came upon the culprit loading fresh meat onto a sled. I shot him. Point blank. No explanation, no excuses, no feelings.

The sad thing was that the sight of the fresh meat made me hungry. I could taste it. I loathed myself for this. So I shot him. I counted eight bodies in all. He had killed some of them in the night. I'd heard the screams. I'd done nothing then. What could I do, alone in the dark? I shivered when I though that a row of cement blocks had saved my life, for I had no doubt that I'd have been on the table if he'd found me. I searched the butcher before I left. The bastard had two cigarettes in a packet. I smoked them both. They made my head light. It was worth it. There was also a bone handled hunting knife in a sheath on his belt. I took it. What had I become? Gathering up my sled I headed towards home.

A movement to my left. Look sharp. A man. Just a spec at the minute but coming my direction. I turn and hurry off, away from my prize. I have an old straw brush head attached to the rear of my sled to turn the snow and cover my tracks. Yes I am paranoid I suppose. Still it has kept me alive these past three years. When I'm far enough away I stop and lie down in the snow. Pulling a white cover over me and the sled. Looking through my binoculars I watch the man approaching. I also scan the tree line. I can see no movement. I am concealed. I feel it. Something is very wrong. Like a bad fairytale. My approaching man is also pulling a sled. There are red and green plastic fuel cans on it. Bundles, carefully wrapped. He's foraging too. I watch him stop at the cigarette packet. He scans the ground. He's looking at my brush marks. He looks directly at me. I know I'm low and white. He looks away. Good, I'm undetected. He stoops and reaches for the cigarettes. Should I break cover and kill him. For God's sake man, what are you saying? For twenty Embassy? I shiver. My thoughts should not be like this.

A sharp crack rings out. For a split second I think it's a rifle shot. I freeze. Away to my right the snow parts and a sturdy branch snaps skyward. A slim steel rope has been underneath the cigarettes; it snares the man's wrist and pulls him off his feet. His body follows the sapling. His arm will be wrenched out of its' socket at the shoulder. His body smashes into the sapling when it is upright and he falls to the ground. From out of nowhere two men appear. I see knives. They huddle around the man. Throat cut. Steel rope removed. He is thrown onto his own sled and pulled off into the forest. It is over in seconds. I think how that could have been me. I know they have no ammunition or they would have shot me when I stopped to view my prize. We are now hunting each other. I watch the men until I can see them no more.

As I pull my sled away in the opposite direction I begin to laugh. I laugh and laugh, imagining what I have just seen as a Television advert. I guess smoking really does kill, mind you; I'd have fought for just one Embassy Red. Now I'm crying and I don't know if it's because of my inaction or my desire for a smoke, and to top it all, it's snowing again.

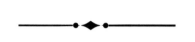

Dedicated to those who fell in the first world war.

7

S·A·D·

GRIMSBY CAMP, ST NICOLAS. I'VE been marching all night just to get here. I'm right fed up I can tell you. Arras, that's where it's closest to. Grimsby camp, it's nothing like Grimsby. My legs ache and my feet are soaked and caked in the mud here. Mud, mud and more mud. Bloody awful, that's what it is, Bloody awful. My men march in behind the Captain. Well he's the only officer left. Both Lieutenants's killed going over the top on the last one. Major killed a fortnight ago along with two full sections. What carnage, that's what it is, bloody carnage. We stop and I call them in to fall out. An officer approaches and my Captain and he salute each other. Bloody officers.

We've been on the front line for two weeks, it was supposed to be one week but the Bosche had a big push so we had to stop longer. We did good too, held them off. Then some bright spark brass hat decided we should counter attack. Crikey, that was how we came to lose so many. Bad idea, bloody bad idea. Still New Year is just around the corner, here's hoping that nineteen seventeen will be better. In the hot food queue we stand in silence, only the muffled sound of mud caked feet shuffling over dry duckboards is audible.

We will eat first. Before we pick a billet or a bunk, before a bath and the issue of a dry, new uniform, we shall eat.

In the bath house I dry my thin, scrawny body on a scratchy towel. I leave the small white cake of soap for the next man in a tin dish hooked on the edge of the bath. At least the water was hot. It is a hive of activity here. Rows on semi naked men either getting into a tin bath, drying themselves and dressing in new uniforms or shaving with the issue cut throat razors after a good lathering up. Trying to use small mirrors that are wet with the condensation of two dozen baths being filled with steaming hot water. Two barbers are shaving faces and heads at the far end of the bath house and two men are burning wet, lice infested uniforms that men have worn for weeks and weeks, outside near the door.

My billet is an old stable that must have forty bunks and camp bed of all sorts erected inside it. Equipment is strewn everywhere as men sleep below blankets in the semi warm for the first time in days. Everything is haphazard, except for the rifles. Cleaned, oiled and stacked in crudely made wooden rifle racks inside the billet. Ready and waiting in case of attack. Tonight we do not need to post a guard. Men who have been on the front line are allowed three nights of freedom. No sentry duty, no watch keeping, no fire warden tasks, just sleep and letter writing, oh and hot food too. Three meals a day, as promised. They taste grand, especially when we been living in trenches, eating cold bully beef and salt tack for days on end. No rum tot at night though, that's kept for the trenches and the officers. Bloody officers.

At eleven o'clock in the pm I was approached by another sergeant. I was smoking my last Senior Service at the side of my billet. I had a sense of foreboding on seeing him walking in my direction. Knowing that he was also staff officer to the Major and the man chosen to delegate unpleasant tasks.

'Sarn Raine', he begins, 'pick eleven men and yourself, just rifles and fall in at five am in the rear stack garden'.

'Very good, can I ask what for?'

'SAD duty.'

'S A D?' I repeat like the greenest recruit.

'SAD,' he snaps, 'Shot at dawn, damn it man. Bloody deserter.'

I feel like I have been slapped in the face. Firing squad, surely not after all my boys have been through. I want to protest and ask that some of the bloody pen pushers or shovel men should be used. Not my boys, for the love of God, not them. He turns to walk away then stops and turns to face me. In a different almost respectful tone of voice he says;

'He's only a lad. I want a proper quick clean job done. Your boys are all crack shots'.

'What did he do?'

'He left his post, Gerry broke through and three sleeping men were killed. They caught him trying to board a boat at Calais, poor sod'.

I nod. He thanks me and marches off. Sometimes I'm glad I'm on the front line. I couldn't do that job. Not for all the tea in China. Returning to my billet I pick eleven other man, good, sturdy, hearts of oak types. All battle hardened and crack shots. Then I drink tea, laced with rum from my own supply. I sleep little.

It's five am and my party are formed up at the stack garden. My Captain has appeared. His eyes cannot look at me. I watch him draw and check his service revolver. This is the fourth time he has checked and re-holstered it.

'Sarn Raine, form the men up'. Says my Captain.

I give the orders in a clear voice but I do not shout. I have no intention of frightening the poor bugger any more than he already is. We smartly march into the small square garden. At the far end is a wooden post. The death post. The last post. I give the orders and we form two ranks. The Captain moves away to my left.

We wait. Then we wait some more. Two military police march in trailing a lad between them. He is semi conscious; I can smell the rum from him as he passes by. Sweet stench of sugar liquor fills my nostrils. One military police man ties him to the post looping the ropes underneath his arms and around the metal hook. An army chaplain who has appeared is helping and praying at the same time. I don't know if he's Catholic or Church of England, I gave up on all that at Vimmy Ridge.

The second military policeman marches over to us, reaching into his pockets I see him draw out the bullets. Some live, some blanks. We will never know if we fired the killing shot. That's the theory, but men such as mine will know. A lighter recoil, a duller report. You know, just the way you know if you put your shoes on the wrong feet or pour custard in your tea instead of milk. I give the command. Again I am firm but not loud.

'Present arms.'

A metallic and wooden clatter.

'Front rank kneel.'

A shuffling of feet.

'Load one round'.

More metallic clicking.

'Make ready'.

The men shoulder their rifles. I see the military police man and the chaplain exit the garden. I am looking down the sights of my Lee Enfield. My hands are trembling. This is wrong. So very wrong. He's only a lad and he's in full British army uniform. My eyes sting as I feel the moisture descending. A misty, salty curtain. Suddenly the lad straightens up and vomits. He is blindfolded and half chokes. His body convulses. He is shaking his head and the blindfold is slipping.

'FIRE!'

My shoulder jerks as the rifle recoils. The early morning report sends birds skyward and makes my ears ring. My Captain, who had shouted the order, runs in he has his pistol out. I see the tremble in his hands. Another shot, duller and quieter than the first volley. He has delivered the coup de gras. Making sure the lad did not suffer, although from the blood seeping from his chest it is apparent my men have been accurate.

'For inspection port arms,' I say.

Walking down the line my Captain checks each chamber is empty. Two live rounds lie on the ground. It appears that not everyone has fired.

'Fall out,' says my Captain and we do.

'Sarn Raine.'

I turn to face him. I know that the men who did not shoot could be court-martialled for disobedience. He nods at the live rounds,

'Better collect those,there's a good chap.'

'II see a tear in his eye too. Gathering up the rounds I shoulder my rifle and walk out of the garden. My men have gone on ahead so I am left to walk with the Captain. A medical doctor and the military police are cutting the lad down. We watch for a few minutes.

'Good idea getting him drunk on rum.,' says my Captain

'Aye sir.'

'God awful waste.'

'Aye sir.'

We halt at the Captains tent.

'Good job, well done Sarn Raine.'

'Thank you sir.'

He goes inside and I walk on. Stopping at a supply wagon I vomit too. Leaning back against the wagon wheel I see the captain. My Captain. Our leader. He is standing at the rear of his tent and is drinking neat whiskey from the bottle. I'm sure he is crying. Wiping my mouth I turn and shoulder my rifle. Someone is whistling. It's a long way to Tipperary. I walk in the direction of my bed and listen to the sounds of a military camp coming alive in the early morning.

Five weeks later my Captain was killed leading a platoon over the top. He won the Military Medal for his action. What a waste. A bloody, mindless waste.

———•◆•———

I guess the stories so far have been, well, heavy.
This is a bit more light hearted and injects some
Ulster humour.

———•◆•———

8

Sanctuary

—— • ◆ • ——

'WHERE'S MY DA?'

'He's in the shed son. In that bloody shed.'

'Thanks Ma.' I open the back kitchen door and stroll down
to the small wooden shed where my father spends most of
his waking hours. As I leave the cement path I cross onto
several paving slabs placed at strange angles, all leading to
the small eight by ten shed. It has been here for as long as I
can remember and my father has always been secretive and
sensitive about it. I know what you are thinking, yes, it is
just a garden shed.

When my brother and I were small we once placed the
lawn mower in it. It was during the great garage clean up
of ninety four. My father came home from work, went to
the shed and shouted and cursed as he trailed the petrol
mower out of his sanctuary. Once we placed empty paint
tins just inside the door. They were chest high. We went off
to university the next day. Mum told us dad went berserk
when he opened the door. He came up the garden carrying

the cans in a bunch in each hand. He looped his fingers through the plastic straps. One can was not quite empty and had spilled Crown emulsion all down his trouser leg. She said he called me a wee bollocks and my brother a bigger bollocks. Although she did say he had to laugh himself when he saw the state he was in.

My brother married and went to live in Australia. I married the following year, in haste and two years later she left me. Now I was home. No house, no job and no wife. I was about to open the shed door when my father flung it wide and greeted me with a hug.

'How are ye?'

'I'm ok Da, I'm ok.'

'So has that bitch left with the Nelson fella then?'

'Aye she has.'

'Good job too.'

'I tried everything Da, family mediation, marriage guidance. Cost me lots.'

'How much?'

'You really don't want to know.'

I step inside the shed and see a second chair has appeared. My father smiles at me.

'I got you that chair son. From our roof space. Try it for comfort.'

I flop into it and it's familiar shape fits me well. It smells of dust and living room. I remember it now as part of a set when I was much younger.

'So the therapy didn't work then?'

'No Da. No not really.'

My father sits down too and pulls out a large wooden block from under the desk. We called them cheeses. They were the rings of wood cut from trees by chainsaw. One big ring was always kept to place smaller rings onto and split with a hatchet for firewood. He scatters a handful of long nails onto the wooden cheese and then produces a hammer. Holding it proudly he starts a nail into the block and then beats it in with extreme ferocity. Grinning he says;

'This is my therapy for you. Just imagine that cheese is Nelsons big head. That big turnip head he has. You can beat away at it when you feel angry or down.'

I stare in disbelief.

'Here,' he says, 'You try.'

I take the hammer and beat in three nails. The last one I really hammer home. I do feel better. How could this be? How could he know this?

'See,' he beams,' See. Knew you'd feel better.'

I begin the long story of my unhappy marriage and the deceit, lies, pain and all the rest of it. He listens for a while and just when there is a pause he leans over to the grey metal filing cabinet in the corner and slides open the bottom drawer. Two tin mugs are produced and two old lemonade bottles. The label on one says 'Paintstripper' and 'Thinners' on the second.

'Clove rock or brandy balls? He asks. Holding a bottle in each hand.

'What?'

'It's crater. Clove rock or brandy balls.'

'Crater', I repeat like a dazed man.

'Aye, poteen.'

'I know what crater is. I just didn't know you drank it Da.'

'How do you think I stuck your ma all these years?' he laughed. I found myself laughing too. Opening the clove rock bottle he pours the pink liquid into the tin mug and reaches it to me.

'Cheers, I never liked that wife of yours and you're better off without her. Good riddance to her and turnip head'.

We sip the smooth liquid which is so easy to drink. It burns all the way down and caresses the body with its warm afterglow. One cup leads to another and I find myself telling him all the intimate details and inner feelings I have been holding onto these past few months. Then a stark noise makes him freeze. He holds his hand up mouthing me to be quiet. Reaching over he closes the door tight and lifts an object from behind it. It is a white plastic box with and aerial and flashing coloured lights.

'What's that?' I ask.

'Baby monitor'.

'What?'

'Baby monitor. The sender is in the hall, hidden behind the flowers so your Ma can't see it. It lets me know when unexpected visitors are in the house en route to the shed. I can close the door, there's a wee bolt on the inside. Most folk think I'm out the back gate and away up the river. I make them none the wiser.'

'Don't you like visitors then Da?'

'Aye, mostly I don't mind but recently it's been Jim from next door, talking about his piles and various operations. Put years on ye. Or that auld Maguire prattling on about the bowlers and how they cheated him out of a place in the nineteen seventy four finals. Did ye ever?'

I nod, expressing my sympathy. More clove rock follows. He produces a flask and we have coffee to accompany the crater. I hear the house phone ringing through the baby monitor and we listen my mother's conversation with Mrs Benson from the church woman's guild or some such. It appears that there is a flower display on tonight and my mother has forgotten about it. My father grins at me.

'Here, if yer Ma's going out we'll get chips from the Golden Fryer because she has no tea on yet.'

I smile. I hear the receiver being replaced and my mother 's footsteps on the laminate floor in the hall. I hear the kitchen door opening and my father turns off the monitor, hiding it on the floor under his chair.

'Straighten up', he says and lifts down one of his hundred or so model aircraft that are strewn around the shed. He's busy gluing a tail fin on when my mother opens the door.

'Albert, I've got to go to the church. There's a flower doo on. There is salad in the fridge for you both, can you sort it out?'

'We'll do that. Have a good night.'

She smiles at me. A mother's smile. A kindly smile. My special smile. Then she is gone. My father sets the model aircraft down and laughs.

'You know I haven't built a model for five years'

He puts his hand into his pocket and pulls out a ten pound note.

'Come on,' he says 'two fish suppers and then we'll return and beat more nails into turnip head.'

Walking up the garden I find myself laughing. He has his arm around me and we walk like father and son, like we did when I was wee and a journey to the chip shop was the Friday night treat. Turning at the gate I gaze back at the shed. I see it as a shed no longer but as a place of sanctuary. A place of therapy. A place of healing. My father looks me in the eye and says;

'You know son there are three things in life I'm thankful for, one is my family, the second is my shed '. There is a pause.

'The third?' I ask.

'Oh the baby monitor. Grand job Isn't it?'

We laugh and laugh as we make our way down the road. It's great to be home.

I sail a lot. I think a lot. Sometimes I sail and think. Is that multitasking I wonder?

9

Strange Shore

— ·◆· —

I PUT THE TACK IN and the Drascombe Lugger swings gently to the port side, settling upright after a few seconds and begins to catch the wind through her bow. We turn, her and I, around Skernaghan point and make way towards Larne harbour. A fine spray breaks over the gunwale and salt water stings my eyes making me squint. I rub them with a cold wet finger making the irritation much worse. Glancing down I find a semi dry cloth and wipe my face properly. When I again look to the front I see that I am now sailing in a thick, swirling mist. Visibility almost zero, I panic for a split second then remember JP's calm voice instructing me, inside my head. His soothing, sensible and logical voice. I react with robot like motion, dropping the main sheet and folding the mainsail I wrap it around the mast holding it fast with a sail tie. I drop the foresail too; pulling the sheets and watching it spin into the furling Genoa. Soon it is all rolled up, like a carpet, safe, sound and catching no wind. I notice that the wind has dropped and so has my speed, one, maybe, one and a half knots.

I keep the sail on the mizzen mast loose hoping that it will steady the boat. As suddenly as the fog appeared it clears. Not fully but enough to allow me to see several yards and the shore on the Islandmagee side. I am sailing to Magheramorne and my safe berth. That's when I see it and I stare in disbelief. A lump in my throat, eyes wide with wonder. A Viking longboat, at least forty feet long, complete with red and white striped sail. A big square sail, I am approaching it from the stern. I can see the steersman standing tall above the crew, leaning on the rudder. I notice that it is lashed to the starboard side with a thick leather strap. Very convincing, a great replica I think. The wind has picked up slightly so I wind out some foresail. I begin to catch up on the longboat. Glancing over I see a row of brightly painted war shields all along the port side of the boat, the crew are rowing in a well practiced, synchronised, motion. They too are in period dress, the pointed helmets with the nose guards and heavy clothing, woollen and animal skin of assorted types. I can see spears and swords too and I can't help feeling that the reconstruction has been a little too well done. They seem to be very heavily armed.

A fat, red headed man looks in my direction. He turns away and a few seconds later several men look over towards me. I raise my hand giving a friendly wave. Two men stand up and then something flies past my head, it just misses me. Another item slams into the mast and spins end over end landing at my feet. It's an arrow. Long and black with a metal tip. A long black arrow head with a barb on both sides. I react dropping my mainsail instantly and at the same time pulling the wooden tiller towards me. The drascombe jibes although more slowly than normal, a gust of wind fills my sail and I begin to pick up speed. Another arrow flies across my stern. I can hear its urgency, the whizz of the wind rushing through the tail feathers. I follow its curved course and see it splash into the sea only a few yards away. I'm pulling out the foresail now, watching it unfurl. It fills with wind almost instantly and we gather more speed.

The longboat is now well away to my starboard side and I am travelling toward the Islandmagee shoreline. That's when I see the rest of the longboats There must be at least ten, all rafted together. I can see Vikings on the shoreline and some further inland. There are several small stone cottages on the upward slopes and three are burning. Black acrid smoke curls skyward, I see men and women running, being chased and cut down by these raiders. My blood runs cold. What is happening here? I suddenly realise that I am fast approaching the shoreline, aware that the Drascombe draws very little water I again tack and change direction. I am now travelling back toward the port and out of the Lough. I am very close to shore, glancing over the side I can see seaweed and wreck in the water. I can feel it scraping the boat, like dead men's fingers, tapping and scratching on the hull and keel.

Movement on my port side catches my eye, it's the longboat. They have turned and are travelling toward me. I see that they have retracted the oars and are sailing, they must be doing close to ten knots, estimating that they will be alongside in a matter of minutes and well within arrow range even sooner I begin to sail in earnest. Sailing like I never have before. I close haul and pull out toward the centre of the Lough. It must be blowing at least a force four. I jibe, allowing the wind to come across my boat from the stern. Now I need more speed so I decide to gullwing. I let the main out to the port side and I feather the fore sail out to the starboard. In effect I have doubled my sail area and with a good tailwind I am soon travelling out of the Lough toward the open sea. Glancing behind me I see the bow of the longboat getting smaller and smaller. My wet hands work the wet sheets they are like slippery fish sliding and skidding through my palms. I steer the rudder with my body as well as whichever hand is free. I must look like a crazy disco dancer swaying and twisting trying to keep the boat steady. I am sweating and still confused. Then all at once I am back in the mist, the wind has stopped and my speed has been taken by the incoming tide. I stop.

What to do next I wonder? Deciding not to tie the sails up in case the longboat appears I drift a while on the tide. Something dark and black looms up out of the mist. My heart skips a beat. It's the number four buoy. It is tilted toward Magheramorne as the incoming tide pushes past it. I can see the rusty ladder on its side leading up to the green navigation light. I drift past it and realise that I am travelling back toward the Vikings. The mist begins to lift. How can this be I wonder, how can there be mist and fog one minute and a force four blowing the next?

The mist lifts completely and my sails flap as the wind fills them gently. I trim with the sheets and we again begin to pick up speed. I strain my eyes through the clearing mist in an attempt to see the raiders and know which direction to take. I see no one. I again sail toward the Islandmagee side as I need to collect wind to gather speed. Now the shoreline is deserted. I see a Fast fisher motorboat on its moorings. No Vikings. No burning cottages. Just some farm houses and the odd modern bungalow with a four by four parked outside. Then the man made island, now a bird sanctuary, near the old cement works and the slipway beyond come into view. My Ford Focus awaits there complete with boatrailer attached. There are lots of other boats moored, I see no one near them, no longboats, no Vikings. I must have been dreaming? I wonder if I am coming down with something. Perhaps a fever, I'm still sweating and my breathing is still laboured. Right, that's it no more cigarettes for me and no more beer either. I think I will go see my doctor and find out why I think I see things.

The Drascombe reaches the slipway and stops with a grinding noise letting me know that she has no more water underneath her bow. I leap out and stroll up the slipway. A short time later the boat is on the trailer and the masts have been taken down, the sails stored and all secured for the short journey home. At my house I park the boat and unhitch the car. I tell my wife of my ordeal and we both laugh. She thinks too much writing and too many late nights are to blame. We come to the logical, grown up's conclusion that I had dozed off and had a wee daydream. I get a scolding for the danger of sleeping while sailing and I promise to be more careful in future.

At eleven thirty I go out to the boat and gather up the sails. Rolling them up carefully I place them in their sail bags. I stow all sheets and pump out any water with the bilge pump. It gurgles and sounds like a child sucking on a straw when the drink container is already empty. The floor of the Drascombe is a wooden slatted affair and the bilge pump hose reaches deep underneath it. The pump is labouring with each pull I make on the wooden handle. I prize up the rear floorboard and reach in to clear whatever is obstructing it. Mostly leaves or weed or old rope cuttings get trapped this low down. My fingers find the long thin obstruction and I free it after a few seconds. I pull it out and hold it up in the full glare of the outside house light. It's an arrow, about a foot long. It is black and has a metal tipped barb on the end. My mouth falls open and I sit down on the lawn grass. Turning the arrow over in my hands I stare in wonderment and disbelief.

This wee story is very special to me. My creative writing tutor gave me a picture and asked me to write about it. It was a Hopper picture of a diner in the USA in the nineteen forties, it is called Nighthawks. I penned the following short story . . . . my very first.

10

Phillies Diner

So who am I? Well, let me say I'm the eyes of the city; the man who tells it like it is. Things are never what you think; take this picture of Phillies diner.

The man sitting on his own with his back to you. Yeah. That's him, the one on the left. He's Frankie. Known as Frankie the fixer. He fixes things or to be more exact, he fixes people. He's from out of town. Mr Caladori has employed him to help sort out a problem. That particular problem is the other man you can see, Leo Escati, or Leo the rat as he has become known these last few weeks.

Leo has been ratting to the feds all about Mr Caladori's money and accounts. What? You want me to spell it out? Ok; Caladoris a mob boss, his moneys dirty and Leo was his book keeper. You guessed it. Frankie is going to fix Leo for Mr Caladori. Now you getting the idea? The broad? Oh, that's Delores, some say she's a hooker, anyway, she's sweet on Leo. Want to look closer?

'More coffee sir?' Ross the waiter asked.

'Yeah' grunted Frankie, all the while his eyes looking down at the counter top.

Ross lifted the glass coffee pot and topped up the white cup.

'What bout you sir?'he asked Leo

'No kid, no thanks'

'Delores?' He gestured with the coffee pot.

'No thanks sweetie.' Delores replied.

Frankie reached into his overcoat pocket and pulled out a silver cigarette case. He flipped it open and put a lucky strike to his mouth, lighting it with silver Zippo. The Zippo had the stars and stripes emblazoned on it. For a split second he could smell the lighter fuel in the Zippo just before he struck flint and it ignited in a sombre yellow glow. Closing the lid he dropped the lighter back into his pocket, pulling deeply on the cigarette he blew out a long column of blue smoke.

Frankie shifted back in his chair allowing his gaze to glance fleetingly at Leo. Yeah, he was going to shoot him alright. After all he'd spent the best part of two days tailing him all over Greenville. On the word of one of his many informers, you know, snitches, he had waited Phillies diner and as promised Leo had arrived a few minutes ago.

Frankie could feel the weight of the Colt 45 pistol in his leather, well worn, shoulder holster, beneath his left arm. Yeah, a model 1911 Colt 45; big; solid. A real mans shooter.

Sure the clip only held seven bullets, but he figured two would do the job. He had wiped the shells clean with a soft lint cloth that morning. Making sure there were no finger prints on them as he loaded the clip. So the cops would find the empty shell cases, so what?

If his information was correct, Leo would walk to his rooms along 147 and Main. There he would turn right along the alley behind Wongs Chinese laundry and onto Central Avenue. Frankie would follow him to the alley and take him right there. Two in the back, close and personal. Yeah, he liked that idea.

'Got a couple of paper napkins Ross?' asked Leo

'Sure'

Ross set them up on the well worn, stained, wooden counter top. Leo and Delores were looking in her red purse. She pulled out a pen and handed it over to Leo. Frankie noticed her long, elegant fingers with the bright red nail varnish. She likes red he thought. Red dress, red purse, red hair and red nails too.

Leo took the pen and began to write on the paper napkin. He slid it across to Delores. She read it and smiled, showing her white slightly crooked teeth. She leaned across and kissed Leo on the cheek.

I'll take her too, thought Frankie, if she leaves with him. One shot; after all who would lament over a dead hooker?

'OK kid,' Leo said to Ross, 'I'm going. See you.'

'Sure Leo,' replied the kid

Leo turned and kissed Delores, a passionate kiss on the lips.

'Goodnight babe.' He said, turning on his heel he walked out of the diner. The cold night air hit him like he was stepping into an ice box. Leo pulled his collar up to keep it out.

In the diner Frankie drained his coffee cup and set it back quietly on the counter top. He walked out into the night and turned up his collar, but for a very different reason. Delores had been lighting a cigarette as Frankie left the diner. She was asking Ross for another refill. Good. The broad was staying. Two bullets only then. That's OK.

Frankie walked with quick deliberation after Leo and soon caught up with him. Staying a few paces behind. They approached the Chinese laundry a few minutes later and Leo made his right turn. So, the snitch was right. Good call. Frankie's right hand moved silently inside his jacket. Opening the well worn brass catch on the holster. He felt the sturdy butt with its wooden grips and drew out the 45. The streets were empty; after all it was 1.40 in the am. He liked this pistol very much. The Colt was already cocked. The gun had a normal safety catch but also had a raised metal plate in the butt. The plate had to be depressed before the gun would fire. This was done by holding the butt in your hand firmly. So Frankie could keep the safety off all the time. Silent. He would not even make the faintest sound from the gun. No sir, all quiet.

Leo was now a few yards along the alleyway proper. His figure was silhouetted by the bright lights at the far end of the short alley.

Frankie stopped and came up into the aim only a few yards behind his victim.

Bang. Bang. Two shots.

They ripped the still night air apart.

Leo spun around.

He saw Frankie, motionless, behind him. Frankie's eyes were wide open and his face was ashen. His right hand slowly opened and the unfired Colt clattered onto the roadway. His knees buckled and Frankie fell, face down, into the gutter.

Delores stood behind him, a pair of red high heeled shoes in her left hand and a small Smith and Wesson .38 in her right.

'You took you're time,' said Leo.

'Had to take these off,' she said, holding the shoes higher. 'Ran all the way in my stocking feet so he would not hear me.'

Leo moved toward her and hugged her. Delores pulled on her red shoes.

'Turned out you were right, he was the man sent for you,' she said, looking at Frankie the fixers' lifeless body.

'Yeah, I've met him before. Couple of years ago in Austin. That's why I wrote 'FOR SURE' on the napkin. I knew he was Caladori's man.'

Both turned and Leo slipped his arm around her waist as they walked back down onto Main.

Like I say, I'm the eyes of this city. Nothing is ever as it appears. It's never in the bag—until it's in the bag. Know what I mean?

11

Who Comes Here?

RAIN RUNS ALONG THE WIDE brim of my hat and drips off onto my great coat. I have my collar turned up, trying to fill that gap at the back of my head where the Stetson finishes and the sheepskin collar begins. A multicoloured Indian blanket is wrapped around me, although it too is soaked and sticks to my leather chaps around my knees and down my shin bone. My chestnut mare picks her way carefully along the steep slopes where I have been trying to track the other horses for two days now. I'm heading toward the old mining camp at Razorback ridge. That's where they will be, sure as eggs is eggs. I can feel it.

My rain has now turned to snow. Small flakes at first. Spinning to earth, all silent and frozen. Then more serious as I complete the short climb and am out from among the trees. More exposed, this is a harsh land in winter. It has no mercy, no quarter is given to travellers. Mother nature is raw and unforgiving here. Death comes to those who ignore the weather or are reckless. The folly or disregard of youth or just plain bad planning by a journeyman has the same consequences in this arena. My snow is deeper now. Settling down in small drifts. Whipped up here and there by a winter wind which is now becoming noticeably stronger.

Men have crossed these mountain ranges since time began. My father and grandfather hunted, trapped and eked out a living on land such as this for a lifetime. It's as if they are riding with me to day. I can see my father, tall in his saddle, wearing that stupid woollen hat my mother knit him, the one with the ear pieces that tie below the chin. He wore that damned hat for decades. I can feel him close by, although he has been gone these many years.

Something on the trail ahead of me brings me back to the here and now. It's a lump in the snow. A lump all white and misshapen, it has a hand sticking out of it. I slip silently off my horse, my hand finding the butt of my Colt Peacemaker. I feel I will not need it. This lump is very still. It's a man. Lying face down, half covered with snow. I see something else too. Blotches of red on the snow. Not fresh but not too old either. Maybe four hours at most. Three big patches of discolouration, as my eyes sweep off to the tree line I see it. A bear. A massive brown bear. It too is slumped in the snow and half covered.

Stooping at the man's body I feel his neck. He is cold. Semi frozen. Looking up I can see only hoof tracks leading off into the forest. His horses are long gone. From his shape and the disturbance on the ground I can only guess he was leading them when the bear attacked. His left side has been badly mauled, again, I can only presume he fended off with his left arm while he drew his old black powder pistol with his right. At any rate he's shot the bear which has then run off, but not far. I guess the damage has been done in the first few seconds of the attack. Without too close an examination I can see his legs are both broken. A frozen pistol and several blankets lie on the ground. A water canteen and several dozen beaver pelts tell me that he has been trapping.

Straightening up I can almost hear my father say, 'Leave him son. Ground too hard to bury him, horse too tired to carry him.' Yeah I think, you got that right. I mount up. As I ride off I mutter a short prayer. Not that I'm much for praying you understand, but I reckon he deserves it. Walking past the dead bear my horse prances sideways, snorting and watching the dead animal. Even in death they are a formidable creature. It's dark eyes stare skyward. Mouth open, tongue lolling out. Snow is falling on it now. Mother nature is re-claiming both the man and the bear. Calling them back to the earth which spawned them. Soon they will be gone from sight. It's an age old battle. Man, the elements, bears and the snow. It is snowing heavily now. At the top of the next rise I stop and half turn in my saddle. I can only see two white humps on the ground. Nature has closed the curtains on this last act in these two creature's lives. The stage is empty. The snow has covered the blood, like blotting paper, drawing it out of the earth. Soaking it up, hiding it from the next traveller. I feel honoured that I have had a glimpse, a snapshot into the last hours of these two players.

Scavengers will pick their bones clean in spring. Storms and rain will wash them. Scatter them. In a short while it will be as if they have never existed.

Looking down, I pick up the trail I had been following. Maybe four more hours to get to the mining camp. Unless I too meet a bear or some other end. My horse walks on, he, like me is part of this barren landscape. We are one and the same. An age old act.

Sitting by my cosy fire at Christmas I was channel hopping on my television. One channel had Bing Crosby and David Bowie singing little drummer boy. On the other channel a family had been reunited with the body of a missing family member who had been murdered many years before and was now located. I locked onto the worn 'Peace' in both instances. Peace for a family at last and peace on earth at Christmas. I wrote this as a result.

12

Peace On Earth

—•◆•—

Come they told me par rum pa pum pum

Our new born king to see par rum pa pum pum . . . .

'So I'm in the warehouse like and Damien comes in. He was our two i/c then, you know, our second in command. He says we've to bring him in like. Bring him and get his confession'.

'Did you bring him in?'

'Aye he was in the back of the motor. He'd had a beating, not a bad one you understand, but a beating all the same. I pushed him onto his knees and Gerry said he wanted his hands clamped to the table like.'

'Clamped?'

'Held with 'G' clamps. I 'G 'clamped his hands to the bench. He squealed a bit so Murph. put tape over his mouth. He knew like, he was a tout you know, like he was. No question. Everyone knew it,'

'Everyone except us.'

'Well that's as maybe.'

. . . . Our finest gifts we bring par rum pa pum pum

. . . . To set before the king par rum pa pum pum . . . .

'So Gerry takes the hammer and breaks his fingers. It was awful, all that blood and squealing. But it was exciting too. Well I was only eighteen you know. So then Gerry gets a wee cassette tape machine and puts a blank tape in it and get's him to confess that he's a tout. Like he was! Definite! Then he plays the confession back and gives the tape to wee Danny and tells him to take it to his ma and drop it through her letter box.'

'So that's how his mother got the news then?'

'I suppose so. So they were all asking him questions like who his handler was and stuff, but he told us nothing more like. He just cried like a wee girl, like tears and sobbing and stuff. His eyes were all red and that and he had no balls like or he would have told us who was running him.'

'If he knew, or was indeed a tout?'

'Then Gerry called me into the back office and set a bag up on the desk. He drew a revolver out of it. A three fifty seven like and six shells. He says I've been picked, like, me. I couldn't believe it like. He tells me to take him to the beach up the coast and do him, then bury him. Tells me to take Luke and big Eddie with me, spades and a pick and all, but says I'm to do him. Me and no one else like. I was well made up.'

. . . . So to honour him par rum pa pum pum

. . . . When we come par rum pa pum pum . . . .

'Away up the coast we stop at a place Eddie had picked out a lot of days earlier. I walked him up the path, just me, Eddie and him, the tout like. I took him on the sand up to the waters edge and made him kneel down. He was quiet like, he knew.'

. . . . Little baby par rum pa pum pum

. . . . I am a poor boy too par rum pa pum pum . . . .

'The other two went into the gorse and began to dig. I think he knew what they were doing. I could hear the scraping and grunting of the pair as they dug down. They were down a fair depth like when they finished.'

'Did you dig?'

'No, no, I was watching the prisoner like. On the beach and that, you know. He was quiet, not begging or nothing like. He was quiet. I think he knew.'

. . . . I have no gift to bring par rum pa pum pum . . . .

. . . . To give a king . . . .

'So I stood behind him and told him if he wanted to pray now was the time like. I was, I was, like, electric, all nervous and excited but scared too. You know?'

'Did he pray?'

'Aye, he did. He asked God to protect his family and stuff. Odd for a tout to ask that.'

'Did you shoot him?'

'I did. Aye I did. He was my first.'

. . . . Shall I play for you par rum pa pum pum

. . . . On my drum par rum pa pump um . . . .

'I walked around his front and shot him in the chest. He looked up at me and he whispered.'

'What did he say?'

'Doesn't matter.'

'I think you need to tell me'.

'He said he forgave me and then he smiled at me'.

. . . . I played my best for him par rum pa pum pum

. . . . Then he smiled at me par rum pa pum pum

. . . . Me and my drum . . . .

'And that was thirty years ago?'

'It was'.

'And you are going to tell us exactly where he is buried so his family can have him back?'

'Aye. I'll take you there.'

'Why now?'

'Well there's peace and all and I've been released like. From gaol like, I done five years of a fifteen stretch you know.'

'What about his family?'

'Well, they'll just have to live with what he done.'

'You mean, what you think he did?'

'Look, I have to think he was a tout. Otherwise I've killed an innocent man and that can't be.'

'You think?'

'Aye.'

'Well there you are then.'

. . . . Peace on earth, can it be?

. . . . Years from now, perhaps we'll see

. . . . See the day of glory

. . . . When men will live in peace . . . . live in peace . . . I pray my wish will come true for my child and your child too . . . . can it be?

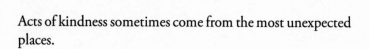

Acts of kindness sometimes come from the most unexpected places.

13

Belfast

———— •◆• ————

Tired eyes stare out at the busy people on the grey rain kissed streets of Belfast. It's early April nineteen hundred and two, the road and wide grey pavements are awash with April showers. A chill wind blows along the thoroughfares and makes the canvas awnings ripple and move above the shop doorways. These awnings were once white or cream but are now Belfast grey. Every now and again a squall of wind blows rain water from the awnings onto the already soaked passersby. Two austere, finely dressed gentlemen, wearing long black raincoats and stovepipe top hats walk briskly past. One carries a fine walking cane with a silver top, they are in deep conversation. Banking matters or investment advice, much too busy to take in the scruffy, thin, drenched young man standing at the mouth of the alley beside the Gentleman's Club. They scurry up the steps to the highly polished heavy oak door and are lost from view. Entering a world of leather chairs, hat and coat stands, hot meals and fine French Cognac.

Across the street the horse trams are making their never ending journeys to the destinations of a city now fully awake. Familiar names displayed on the front, proudly announcing where this tram will rest, Divis, Antrim Road, Ligoniel. Bay and black drenched shire horses with their heavy hooves and firm hind quarters trail the trams full of citizens along the soaked streets. Waiting for their masters to call a halt to their toil and reward them with a canvas nosebag full of oats and hay. Their masters in turn wait for Friday when their masters reward them with an envelope containing shillings for the weeks work. The unbroken cycle of work and reward continues.

The young man leaves the haven of his alleyway and begins to walk toward the City Hall. He limps from the unhealed wound on his left leg, it shall heal with time, they told him. He trails the unwilling limb step after step as he waits to cross the street. A smartly dressed Constable strolls past, his cape cascading the torrent toward the footpath, He has bushy whiskers and a fine moustache and is tall and slim. On his head sits a Belfast night hat with its grand Royal Irish Constabulary badge well displayed, the rain water drips from the rim of this fine helmet, onto the cape and beyond. The Constable nods. Our young man nods back.

'Have you hurt a leg sir?' enquires the Constable.

"I have officer,' the young man hears his own voice and is startled by it. He has now stopped and is talking for the first time in days. Three women, bundled up in heavy clothes push past. They look accusingly at the young man and begin to whisper after they pass. Gossip thrives in this city, same as all cities, could he have murdered someone. A girl maybe, or did he rob an old lady, perhaps he robbed and murdered. Oh! If they could just read about it in the paper, the News Letter, then they could tell all their friends that they saw him being arrested. What news that would be.

'Have you any money on you sir. Or a place to live?'

'No officer. I am trying to get home to Randalstown. I've been away . . . ' his voice trailed off as if exhausted by the short walk.

'I see. I can arrest you under the Vagrancy Act if you have no money. At least that way you would get a bite to eat.'

'I am just home from the army, sir. The fifth Royal Irish Lancers. We've been fighting the Boers in Tarkastad, I got wounded at the Orange River, shot in my leg.' Again his voice trailed off. He produced a crumpled, discharge letter from the army high command and the policeman read it quietly to himself.

The Constable pulled a thruppence from his pocket and slipped it into the young mans hand. With a wink he said in a loud voice;

'Very good sir, there is a tea house on the corner of Wellington Place may be able to assist you. Good day.' With that he strolled off, back to the wet beat and the search for suitable shelter.

So the grey clouds lifted for a short while over Belfast and the young man's grey cloud lifted too with this act of human decency. From the corner table in the tea house he watched the pedestrians again scurry to and fro in their busy lives.

This time he was dry on the outside and wet and warm inside. Examining his change on the wooden table top he realised that he had enough for a bus trip to Antrim, from there it was only two hours walk home, even with this leg.

The sun began to shine on Belfast once more, just as it had when Belfast first became a town and just as it would when it would no longer be a city.

14

Butterfly

• ◆ •

I'T'S ELEVEN A.M. AND TIME for tea. Always at eleven, you could set your watch by it. Eleven and the fat lady appears pushing the trolley with the silver tea urn sitting astride it like a silver chimney stack. Dispensing tea to all and sundry. Heavens above, a nuclear blast could wipe out most of the world and this fat heifer would still enquire as to the tea situation. I can hardly bear it. I loathe and detest this nursing home and the fact that I am stranded here like an old car left in a scrap yard.

Its eleven twenty and I have finished the cup of hot, weak, liquid that passes for tea. The conservatory doors are open and a stunning white butterfly flutters past. I think it may be a Cabbage White. What a horrid name for such a graceful visitor. I watch in silent amazement as it settles on the edge of my tea tray. Sitting high on dainty thin legs, I see it fold its wings back. Now it takes on a different shape and the white colour deepens. The edges of its wings are green. How that takes me back. A green and white butterfly;

It is nineteen forty two and I'm in Ireland on home leave from my regiment. I am a young second Lieutenant in the Irish Guards. It is May and I am sitting in the Grand Central hotel, in my native Belfast. I am waiting to meet my boyhood friend's sister Anne McCreevy. Reading a copy of the News Letter I am trying to look cool and calm but in reality my heart is pounding like a drum. I see the restaurant manager as he walks to and fro seating the newly arriving diners and ensuring hand written menus are freely issued to each. God alone knows why as everything is rationed. To-days menu has no starter listed and only three main courses; Ham and eggs or one lamb chop or a spam fritter. All with boiled potatoes and carrots. Desert is a choice of Ice cream or rice pudding. Still it is better than the rations I have been living on in the North African desert. Spam features there too, I think it is the cement that is holding our nation together at this particular time. Spam. Great Britain would collapse without it.

A familiar voice speaks to me;

'Alan, how nice to see you.'

It is Anne. How? She has approached me and I have been so engrossed in my reading I have not noticed. I flush with embarrassment, I feel my neck and face burning red and I spring to my feet.

'Anne, it's great to see you. How have you been?'

'Oh fine. If you can be fine with the war and all that.'

I am stunned at her beauty. Tall and slim with long flowing auburn locks, green eyes and full red lips. We sit and she produces a packet of Gallaghers Greens from her handbag.

'Wait', I say 'have one of these instead'.

I produce twenty Lucky Strikes that an American Captain gave me for fixing him up with a lift in my jeep from the docks in Belfast to his camp at Langford Lodge near Crumlin. We had shared the same hospital ward for three weeks and had become friendly.

'Lucky Strikes', she replies with an excited tone in her voice.

'Got them from a yank.'

I reach the packet to her.

'Keep it, I can always get more'.

'Nylons too?' she enquires, holding out her long, slender leg. Anne giggles as she twists her foot in a circular motion before crossing her legs again.

'Sorry, no nylons.'

She pulls a pout and makes a child like face. Stockings are like gold dust at the minute.

We order and eat and catch up with all the latest gossip. I watch her smoke and drink. I try to catch all her feminine movements and delicate motions. There is something so innocent and child like in her. I am drawn in and I realise that I am indeed falling for her all over again. We have written to each other since I left Belfast in nineteen forty. Written for two years. She has been my lifeline, my saviour, my sanity and my solace for all that time. She tells of her new job in the City hall and of the air raid shelters and equipment that she must list and catalogue every week. I steer the talk away from my posting and the desert heat and sand and the bloody massacre that was Tobruk and how it happened again at El Alamein.

All too soon the meal is over and we must leave. I produce the two tickets that I have bought for an evening show at the Opera House. As there is still a few hours to kill before the show we decide to take a walk through the streets.

Outside the hotel she puts her right arm underneath mine and holds my left hand with both her hands. We walk and talk; she rests her head on my shoulder. I can smell her perfume and it intoxicates me. I shall remember it forever, lilac. We cover every single subject that anyone could possibly speak about. All except the main one. Her brother Edward. Finding a summer seat we sit and I place my arm around her shoulder. Two years ago such behaviour would have drawn unwanted attention. Would have been frowned upon. Would have set tongues wagging. Now it could be seen all over cities in Britain and Belfast was no different. Men home on leave held the hands of their sweethearts in public, aye, and kissed too. War does funny things to people and breaks the old barriers down. Then she dropped it onto me;

'Did Edward suffer do you think?'

'No, I don't think he did.'

'Did they have an army service for him?'

'Yes. I was at it.'

'Alan,' she said after a pause.

'Yes'.

'I love you.'

'I'm glad because I love you too.'

We kissed then and there. Out in the public eye. I did not care as I knew that I would be leaving soon to return to my unit. I looked into her emerald green eyes and my heart was truly lost forever. We sat for ages without speaking, just holding each other and watching the world go by. I had never felt this way about anyone. I still never have. It was a feeling that I always had when I was with her and a feeling I have never forgotten. Some things cannot be replicated and that feeling of love, of trust, of completeness is one of them.

Anne had her gas mask wrapped up in a brown paper box and it was sitting at her feet. A cabbage white butterfly landed on it and stood on its dainty, spindly legs. It folded its wings back and took on a different shape. We both watched it for what seemed like an age. Early for a butterfly in May. Then it fluttered its wings in the breeze and was gone. Just like that. No warning, no goodbyes, it was gone. After the evening performance at the Opera house I walked her home and we said our good nights. It must have taken me forty five minutes to complete the goodbye ritual. On the bus on the way back to my depot I scribbled a few lines on my programme to remember this day. It was dark and hard to see but my eyesight was better then. The blackout was in full swing, no lights anywhere, even the bus headlights were covered with only a small slit to allow light out. War creates pretty dismal conditions for everyone.

My Cabbage White stirs. Opening his wings in one graceful, easy movement he is gone. My fat tea lady approaches with her thick ankles and gravel voice. Lifting my tea cup. I watch my butterfly circle high above before he finds the open door and freedom. Farewell my white and green friend. I watch the place where I last saw him. Willing him to return, but in vain. Life is a collection of moments such as this, memories and images held and remembered. Items and things recollected and savoured then the loneliness of a vapour lost, emptiness that not even time can replace. A butterfly, white and green and gone.

When we are children we all play and get along pretty well with each other. There comes a time, however, when we seem to change. This story tries to capture the complexity of that human condition.

15

The Wake

————— •◆• —————

It's three o'clock in the afternoon. A winter's day in the deep Ulster countryside. Mid Ulster to be exact. I park my Ford Cortina in the small stone lay-by just at the end of the lane. A bitter wind bites into my bones as I climb out of the car, my ear lobes tingle with the chill. Reaching into the back seat I pull out my green waxed cotton coat and a woolly black hat. Finding only one glove, I curse under my breath. I'll just keep my hands in my pockets then, if only I could.

I gather up the assortment of buns and cakes my mother gave me, it's in a pastry box. Fresh from O'Neill's home bakery in the town. Her and my father will go to the funeral tomorrow. I will be away in Scotland, to the farm machinery auction that Willie John had arranged on Saturday. It was the day John died. To-day was Monday. I look at the pure white string wrapped and tied around the pastry box. I wonder how many years home bakeries have used these white thin cardboard boxes tied with cord. Ever since I was a wee boy I suppose. I am twenty five now.

My leather soled brogues slip and skip over the stones and cobbles on the long laneway. I hold the pastry box in front of me carrying it the way a man carries an unexploded bomb or the last Ming vase in Christendom. I feel the pastries slide from side to side. I imagine Mrs O'Neill's face when she opens it and finds the train wreck inside. Slowing my pace I readjust my grip on the box. This lane is nearly a mile long. I played here as a boy. Mostly with John O'Neill. We were inseparable as children. We were always playing, both attending the same primary school. John was a Roman Catholic and I was not. I suppose the change happened when we went to different secondary schools. Only meeting up now and then, mostly in the town. John's friends were distant towards me and although he tried they never came around to my acceptance. Still, he'd come and help on our farm at the end of every June. We'd ruck hay, bale it, cut silage and feed cattle together. It was a pity that we grew apart. He was a nice lad and I loved him dearly as a friend.

In the summer when he was seventeen he learned to drive. Borrowing his dad's old Escort he took me to town one Saturday evening. We cruised about, admiring the girls and trying to catch glimpses of ourselves as we passed the shop windows. It was an old Escort but to us it was a Mercedes. We were cruising. I drove the old farm Land Rover when I needed to. I could hardly cruise in it. It had straw and hay on the floor and a smell inside it of wet dog and sheep dip. Not good for picking up girls. So we cruised in John's car when we could. Stopping for chips that evening John went to get his cigarettes from the car. I was left inside the chippy. Coming out the door carrying my American burger and chips I was confronted by a group of boys all talking to John.

Everyone stopped talking when I appeared and a very frosty atmosphere descended. I was ignored despite the fact that I said hello and was jovial and polite. One boy continued his conversation with John in Irish. I remember everyone laughing as I got into the car. John stayed talking with the boys until he'd finished his cigarette. Their conversation continued in Irish. I did not speak it so I felt that I was not allowed to hear what they were saying.

Something changed that evening. We ate our chips in silence and although I tried conversation there was none to be had. That was the last time I was in his company. Twice more I met him in town, always with the same group of boys. Twice he ignored my waves and friendly gestures. So I left school and worked on the farm. I drove the Land Rover whenever I could and got on with farming life. John had been serving his time in a garage in the town. I met the other mechanic one day and upon enquiring about John was told he'd been sacked. Well, to be exact he'd stopped attending and after three weeks the garage owner sent a letter telling him not to return. It was after a police patrol was ambushed and shot up close to the town that more news emerged. John and two other lads were missing. I was slow at assembling all the facts. John was 'on the run' as they say in Ulster.

As I approach the front door at his parent's house I see that parking at the road was a good idea. There are three cars and a van abandoned in the yard. It's not a big yard, so these vehicles fill it to capacity. I'd rather walk in than drive in and have to try to reverse out. Good choice. My rough hands knock the front door. It's a solid wooden door with the blue paint peeling here and there. All the blinds are pulled. The house looks as if it's in mourning too. His sister Bernadette opens the door.

'Ah Davy,' she half whispers,' Sure it's good to see you. You are very welcome.'

'Bernie, I was sorry to hear about John'.

'Come in, come in'.

I follow her inside and allow my eyes to grow accustomed to the dark, smoky atmosphere. John's father smoked a pipe and it seemed he had been working overtime. I was almost over powered by the rich, aromatic smell of Walnut Plug or Warhorse. Everyone was in the kitchen with its AGA stove and wicker basket of peat stacked beside it. It was warm and as welcoming as I'd remembered. The smell of the tobacco, peat smoke and baked soda bread took me back to a better time, long ago.

His mother arose from the fireside and greeted me with outstretched arms.

'It's good to see you,' she said.

'Mrs O'Neill, I'm sorry for your trouble,' I whisper and then I give her the box I have been attached to for the last half hour.

'My Ma sent those for you, she will be at the service tomorrow. Her and my Da.'

'Thank her for me son,' she says. Then turning to Bernadette she orders tea for me and her husband. I shake hands with him too and say how sorry I am. I am too. Genuinely sorry. I have fond memories of us playing nearby as children.

'Would you like to see him?' asks Mrs O'Neill. I sense looks from Bernadette to her father and then from them both to Mrs O'Neill. There is a static, atmospheric silence. It's as if everyone wants to speak at the same time but someone has pushed the pause button.

'Aye,' I hear myself say. 'I'd like to say goodbye. If that's OK?'

'He's not on his own . . . ' begins Bernadette.

'There's a couple of lads with him . . . . ' stammers Mrs O,Neill.

'Oh for heaven sake, 'says John's father,' you know how he died Davy. Are you alright with that?'

I nod. Bernadette takes me through the parlour and I follow her upstairs. At the bedroom door she pauses.

'Wait here,' she says. I wait.

She disappears into the room closing the door behind her. I seem to wait for an eternity before the door opens. Walking in I am confronted by the coffin in the centre of the room. The bed has been removed and the coffin sits on the chrome trestles left by the undertaker. Two men stand to attention. One at each side if the coffin. They wear white shirts, black ties and black trousers. Both have dark glasses on and black berets. I don't know them. On their left arms are small green white and gold armbands. I'm startled but strangely not afraid. Bernadette grabs my arm and we walk over slowly. John is that strange pale, almost blue colour the dead become. His eyes are closed and he is covered up to his chin in lace and white shroud net. I feel tears. I bite my lip and try not to blink. His face looks peaceful. I lift my hand and reach out to touch his forehead. A glance from one of the honour guard stops me. Bernadette is squeezing my hand tightly. I withdraw my hand. These men are his friends now, not me. Turning to go I notice a chair with a black beret and gloves on it. They are sitting above a neatly folded flag. I recognise it as the Starry Plough.

Back in the kitchen I drink my tea and we talk of old times. Pranks we played on the farmers and girls we chased in the old Escort. I remember cowboys and Indians and great battles in John's yard. Bows and arrows and silver Lone |Star pistols with caps curling out of them when we fired. I can almost hear them. We rode imaginary horses across the fields to my father's farm where we would get our sausage and beans from my mother before a TV treat of the Lone Ranger or the Virginian. Cowboys. It seems John got to play cowboys for real.

Getting up to leave I pull on my coat. Bernadette helps me with the zip. A year younger than me we have always been close. A scrape at the front door brings silence from all in the kitchen. Opening slowly a tall man lets himself in. He brings a blast of winter cold with him and something else. A chill, an atmosphere. Looking directly at me I recognise him as the boy who talked to John at the chip shop that evening. He is older now and I have not seen him in this area for several years.

'Who are you?' he asks.

'This is Davy, he's a neighbour come to pay his respects.' Interjects Bernadette

'I live close by', I say 'I ran about with John when we were wee'. I hold out my hand to shake. It's ignored.

'John?' questions the man 'Who's John.'

I'm dumbfounded and begin to explain when he cuts me short with a raised voice.

'Oh you mean Sean. There are no John's here; it's a foreign name, an English name.'

I turn to John's mother and once again say that I am sorry for her loss. She shakes my hand and I notice hers is trembling. As I leave I feel the man's gaze stays with me.

'Not just her loss,' he says, 'Irelands loss, he was a good volunteer'.

I hurry out the door. Hearing footsteps I half turn and am greeted by Bernadette. A sigh lets her know of my relief.

'Take no notice,' she says, putting her arm through mine, 'You are welcome anytime and you know that.'

'What happened him?' I ask.

'Ah, he got involved in the war on the British I suppose. Those boy's filled his head with nonsense and he began hating everyone. On Friday night he was out near the Enniskillen border and was on some operation or other.

Anyway, there was a trap and the army shot him. It was on the news, didn't you hear.'

'No.' I lied.

'It said on the news that terrorists were laying an ambush for police when SAS soldiers attacked. Two terrorists had been killed and one captured' Bernadette continued, 'Our John was one of the dead.'

There was a silence. Bernadette looked at me;

'At least my mother will know where he is now,' she said, 'These last few years he has come and gone at all hours, away for weeks with no word or contact.'

Stopping at the start of the lane she kissed my cheek.

'It was great to see you, please call again.'

'I will.' I reply 'I promise.' With that she turned and walked back towards the house. I was alone, in the cold wind, facing the long lane. I walked in the fading light.

As I neared the end of the lane I stopped at the old black metal gate. Leaning on it for a minute I gazed across the fields. For a split second I imagined I could see two boys running away from me. One had a cowboy hat at the back of his head, held on by a white string. Wearing a waistcoat, with an empty holster bouncing on his thigh, firing his cap gun and skipping as if he were on a horse. The other was slightly in front of him wearing a cardboard headband that had two feathers pointing skyward. He had a small wooden bow in one hand and three arrows in the other. The arrows were yellow and slim, with red rubber suckers on one end and black plastic feathers on the other. I could hear them shout and whoop as they raced to save the wagon train. I knew soon they would be at my mother's table eating their cowboy suppers.

Then the mist closed around them and they were gone. I looked at the gorse and weeds standing proud against the on coming winter. With my hand I wiped my eyes. Those were better days in a more innocent time. Climbing into my car, I turn the key and the engine coughs into life. As I drive off I find I am wiping my eyes again although I fear it is a losing battle.

———◆———

This last story, is the last story. I often wondered what became of the little girl.

———◆———

16

The Nick of Time

———•◆•———

IT IS SUNDAY AND IT is a late turn of duty for me. I am with Colin in the Vauxhall Omega estate motorway car. It is the main vehicle or the 'Motorway Proper' car as we know it. We carry a vast amount of kit in the rear. There are sixteen orange and white plastic motorway cones, two first aid boxes, eight sequential blue lamps complete with a charging base. Ten yellow lights known as 'Tildawns', two breaking bars or crowbars, a towrope, a massive hand lamp and lots of rolled up road signs and metal stands. They are grey with blue detachable logos on the front saying police road closed or police accident. There are direction arrows too and road closed logos, all to help the motorists. Traffic police receive lashings of training, every time we turn around someone is on a course or just returned from one. We can close the motorway in minutes in a slick, well practiced action. Even the five lane carriageway travelling into Belfast, no problem. Rush hour, yes rush hour too. No worries. Ask and it shall be closed.

I'm driving and I am going towards Belfast having just left our base at Antrim. I'm not long returned to traffic having spent some time in the police motor driving school as an instructor. I liked teaching and always loved driving but I missed the closeness of the traffic section and the action. I always missed the action. Car chases, joyriders, rushing to help other police. The wailing sirens and flashing blue lights. I suppose I must enjoy being the centre of attention. Perhaps it's because I'm an only child? No, I just like driving fast, really, really, fast.

I'm on the five lane section now. The M2 foreshore as we call it. Colin draws my attention to a man running along the nearside lane waving his arms over his head. He appears to be quite frantic, waving and waving. Arms like a windmill. We pull over and he rushes to us.

'Help she's not breathing. Please help she's only a few weeks old.'

I see a car on the hard shoulder several yards in front. Colin debuses and runs with the man to the parked vehicle. I have my window down and can hear a woman screaming. Then I see her emerge holding a small baby. She is cradling it gently in her arms. The child is blue. I grab the radio and press the button;

'Uniform uniform this is Tango eight zero urgent message over.'

'Go ahead' says the ever calm BRC voice.

'We are M2 south box bravo one. We have an infant who has breathing difficulties. Where is nearest A&E who are receiving. Over?'

'Stand by traffic callsign,' his voice smooth like liquid honey.

Colin's now back at the car with the mum and dad and the baby. He gets them into the back seat and he kneels in the front with his back to the windscreen. He is bent over the seat working with the child. I can hear the mother sobbing loudly and I race off the hard shoulder like Michael Schumaker. Soon her sobs are lost in the roar of the three litre, six cylinder engine and the sirens wailing song. First gear right to the red line on the rev counter then second gear. Fifty, sixty third gear then the radio goes;

'Tango eight zero from uniform.' I grab the mike and keep accelerating. I shout;

'Send over.'

'Rodger the Mater hospital is closest to you and receiving. I have alerted them they will have someone on standby, over.'

'Rodger.' I shout letting go of the microphone. It springs out of my hand as the curly wire retracts it back to the main set. I throw another gear into the Omega and notice we are travelling at ninety miles per hour. Down the ski slope towards Nelson Street, hard braking for the red traffic lights. I'm not stopping but I still have to be a lot slower for the junction. They change at the last second and I catapult through them and on to the second set at Little Georges Street.

'Hurry Dave hurry,' says Colin.

'Please hurry, please,' says the father who has now calmed slightly. I cross the junction at the bottom of the Westlink and don't want to think about my speed. I'm travelling very fast. At the North Queen Street junction I again slow and when I see it clear I power on watching the traction control light flicker orange. This vehicle is amazing. In earlier days that would have been a slide and I would have been steering forever to correct it.

Now I'm at the junction where all the traffic lights are red. Clifton Street. All the lanes have cars in them so I make a decision to wrong side the traffic island and go through the red lights against the oncoming cars. I slow down. I'm still doing forty. Is it too fast? I don't have time to change my mind. The oncoming cars stop. I find a gap and I'm through and gone. Third gear, I feel the rev limiter cutting in and I feed fourth to the greedy engine. Now I can see the roundabout at Carlisle Circus. It's teeming with vehicles. I am approaching it at eighty. No that can't be right? Can it? I'm already there. An oncoming Ulsterbus driver has seen the blue lights flashing, announcing my arrival. He is sympathetic to my plight. He must be wondering the same as me, are we going to make this?

He pulls his bus across the lanes at the roundabout blocking it for me. He has stopped the traffic. He is a lifesaver. Now I'm in the roundabout and I know my speed is very high. Will we spin off? Will we crash? The dashboard lights up with the traction control light again. Even the Omega is wondering what is going on. I can almost hear it ask do you even have a drivers licence you maniac? We exit the roundabout and I hear the clatter as the equipment rolls from side to side behind the wire cage in the rear of the car. At last I see the A&E signs and I pull up right at the door. As if by magic a doctor and a nurse appear complete with a small Tupperware box on wheels for the infant. Colin goes with the parents. There is a lot of fussing and confusion in the hallway. I pull the Omega forward and park up. I pick the microphone from the passenger's footwall and press the button again.

'Uniform uniform from Tango eight zero arrival at Mater over.'

'Rodger' says honey voice and then adds 'That was three minutes. Well done over.'

I can't speak and I decide I will exit the car. My legs won't hold me up. They shake. I look like a fat Bambi as I steady myself against the front wing of the vehicle. I see people going to and fro around the hospital car park. I wobble my may round to the front of the car. A small man walks past with his wife. I see him look at me then he turns to her and says;

'See the state of that peeler. He must be full drunk like. It's a bloody disgrace know what I mean.'

Colin returns and laughs at the state of me. We watch the thin trail of smoke curl up from the glowing brake discs and listen to the plink plink sound the cooling engine makes.

'She's going to be OK Dave,' he beams. 'Doctor says she choked. They'll probably keep her in I imagine. Poor wee soul.'

I nod.

'Will you drive Colin?'

'Aye OK mate'.

We get in the car and pull away a lot more sedately. More driving Miss Daisy than warp factor nine Mr Sulu.

Back at Antrim Colin rings the hospital and gets details on the parents so we can follow up. The wee girl was doing fine but as he suspected they were keeping her in overnight. A few weeks later we received a lovely letter from her father who was relieved. He thanked us lots and said he was impressed with the driving standards of the traffic officer. He should have been sitting up front where I was!! Impressed was not a word I would have chosen. Dangerous or outrageous yes, that would have been acceptable but not impressed.

I have often wondered what became of the little girl and over the years I lost her contact details. Policemen are supposed to take an all in a day's work attitude, yet sometimes you cannot help but wonder. I was also forever in the bus drivers debt and sorry that I could not thank him in person. People watch me driving through the city and some ask me why I always hold back and allow busses to pull away from the bus stops. I smile and never say why, but I always do.

Glossary

ATO   Bomb disposal team

Callsigns.   Police term for vehicles or persons deployed on duty.

Crater.   Slang term for poteen or illegal home brewed liquor.

Debus   police term meaning to leave vehicle

ETA.   Radio term for estimated time of arrival.

Geordies.   Slang term for persons from North East of England.

Provos.   Provisional IRA

Ruger.   Pistols and rifles manufactured by Sturm Ruger in the United States of America.

SA80   Issue British army rifle, still in service.

SLR.   Self Loading Rifle, British Army issue in the nineteen eighties.

Also available by David Moore:
The Abbot

The Abbot, tasked by his paymasters to recover an aluminium case. Mr Marc, an MI5 operative and part of the CTO, black operations, also on the hunt for the case. Both killers, both highly trained, driven and motivated.

Jenny, an MI5 science officer, who falls in love. Mr Jay an ex SAS soldier now CTO and working in Ulster. All brought together in the maelstrom of post peace process Northern Ireland. Working from a safe house in the sleepy town of Ballyclare, in County Antrim.

A blistering, action packed journey through the province with shootings, double cross and intrigue as Counter Terrorist Operations (CTO) meet enemies old and new in an attempt to stop a terrorist outrage.

Who is the toughest . . . . Who is the strongest . . . . Who is the Tall Man?

Lightning Source UK Ltd.
Milton Keynes UK
UKOW051432191011

180578UK00001B/28/P

9 781467 000963